"You could take me to the dance."

Jed frowned ferociously, as if her words were a surprise. "I don't mix business and pleasure."

Beth wanted to ask him which he considered her to be, but she didn't. She wouldn't like the answer. "Since we both know you'd only be doing it to protect my reputation, I don't think it would hurt." No need to mention she'd faced these kinds of situations before without a date.

He rubbed the back of his neck, then looked at her again. "I suppose I could, as long as you understand there's nothing personal."

There was something personal, all right, Beth thought. Jed just didn't know it. Yet.

An unexpected inheritance changed their lives... but would love be their ultimate reward?

On sale June 2000: NEVER LET YOU GO
(Silhouette Romance #1453)
On sale July 2000: THE BORROWED GROOM
(Silhouette Romance #1457)
On sale August 2000: CHERISH THE BOSS
(Silhouette Romance #1463)

Dear Reader,

From the enchantment of first loves to the wonder of second chances, Silhouette Romance demonstrates the power of genuine emotion. This month we continue our yearlong twentieth anniversary celebration with another stellar lineup, including the return of beloved author Dixie Browning with *Cinderella's Midnight Kiss.*

Next, Raye Morgan delivers a charming marriage-of-convenience story about a secretary who is *Promoted—To Wife!* And Silhouette Romance begins a new theme-based promotion, AN OLDER MAN, which highlights stories featuring sophisticated older men who meet their matches in younger, inexperienced women. Our premiere title is *Professor and the Nanny* by reader favorite Phyllis Halldorson.

Bestselling author Judy Christenberry unveils her new miniseries, THE CIRCLE K SISTERS, in *Never Let You Go.* When a millionaire businessman wins an executive assistant at an auction, he discovers that he wants her to be *Contractually His*...forever. Don't miss this conclusion of Myrna Mackenzie's THE WEDDING AUCTION series. And in Karen Rose Smith's *Just the Husband She Chose,* a powerful attorney is reunited in a marriage meant to satisfy a will.

In coming months, look for new miniseries by some of your favorite authors. It's an exciting year for Silhouette Books, and we invite you to join the celebration!

Happy reading!

Mary-Theresa Hussey

Mary-Theresa Hussey
Senior Editor

Please address questions and book requests to:
Silhouette Reader Service
U.S.: 3010 Walden Ave., P.O. Box 1325, Buffalo, NY 14269
Canadian: P.O. Box 609, Fort Erie, Ont. L2A 5X3

NEVER LET YOU GO

Judy Christenberry

Silhouette

R O M A N C E™

Published by Silhouette Books

America's Publisher of Contemporary Romance

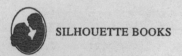

SILHOUETTE BOOKS

ISBN 0-373-19453-6

NEVER LET YOU GO

Copyright © 2000 by Judy Christenberry

This edition published by arrangement with Harlequin Books S.A.

® and TM are trademarks of Harlequin Books S.A., used under license. Trademarks indicated with ® are registered in the United States Patent and Trademark Office, the Canadian Trade Marks Office and in other countries.

Visit Silhouette at www.eHarlequin.com

Printed in U.S.A.

JUDY CHRISTENBERRY

has been writing romances for fifteen years because she loves happy endings as much as her readers do. She's a bestselling writer for Harlequin American Romance, but she has a long love of traditional romances and is delighted to tell a story that brings those elements to the reader. Judy quit teaching French recently and devotes her time to writing. She hopes readers have as much fun reading her stories as she does writing them. She spends her spare time reading, watching her favorite sports teams and keeping track of her two daughters. Judy's a native Texan, but has been temporarily transplanted to Arizona.

IT'S OUR 20th ANNIVERSARY!
We'll be celebrating all year,
Continuing with these fabulous titles,
On sale in June 2000.

Romance

#1450 Cinderella's Midnight Kiss
Dixie Browning

#1451 Promoted—To Wife!
Raye Morgan

AN OLDER MAN

#1452 Professor and the Nanny
Phyllis Halldorson

The Circle K Sisters

#1453 Never Let You Go
Judy Christenberry

The WEDDING AUCTION

#1454 Contractually His
Myrna Mackenzie

#1455 Just the Husband She Chose
Karen Rose Smith

Desire

MAN of the MONTH

#1297 Tough To Tame
Jackie Merritt

#1298 The Rancher and the Nanny
Caroline Cross

MATCHED IN MONTANA

#1299 The Cowboy Meets His Match
Meagan McKinney

#1300 Cheyenne Dad
Sheri WhiteFeather

 the Baby Bank

#1301 The Baby Gift
Susan Crosby

#1302 The Determined Groom
Kate Little

Intimate Moments

 The WILDES of WYOMING

#1009 The Wildes of Wyoming—Ace
Ruth Langan

 The Marrying McBrides

#1010 The Best Man
Linda Turner

#1011 Beautiful Stranger
Ruth Wind

#1012 Her Secret Guardian
Sally Tyler Hayes

#1013 Undercover with the Enemy
Christine Michels

#1014 The Lawman's Last Stand
Vickie Taylor

Special Edition

#1327 The Baby Quilt
Christine Flynn

#1328 Irish Rebel
Nora Roberts

#1329 To a MacAllister Born
Joan Elliott Pickart

 A Family Bond

#1330 A Man Apart
Ginna Gray

 DESERT ROGUES

#1331 The Sheik's Secret Bride
Susan Mallery

#1332 The Price of Honor
Janis Reams Hudson

Chapter One

"Where have you been?" Abby Kennedy asked her sister Beth, meeting her at the door. "You said you'd be back over an hour ago."

A frown on her forehead, Beth moved into the living room. "Flat tire," she said succinctly. The Circle K ranch, their home, was in the lower panhandle of Texas, an hour from the city of Wichita Falls. Tumbleweed, twenty miles away, was the nearest town where she could get a tire fixed. "Did anyone come to see me?"

Jedadiah Davis stood in the shadows of the living room, staring at the beautiful young woman who'd finally returned, after he'd waited for more than an hour.

He should have been prepared for her beauty. After all, her sisters, Abby and Melissa, were both lookers. But something about Elizabeth Kennedy grabbed at him more than both of her sisters put together. Bad sign.

Besides, he wasn't sure he was interested in a rich lady for a client. He'd agreed to meet with her, but he hadn't made any promises. Word had gotten out that these ladies were wealthy. He'd given the missing sister the benefit of the doubt, but after waiting for an hour, he was fed up.

Fed up, or scared to death of getting close to her, his inner voice teased. She was young, fresh, rich and beautiful. What did she want with barrel racing? She didn't need that particular spotlight to be noticed.

"Mr. Davis is here. He said he had an appointment," Abby said, gesturing in his direction.

Beth stepped forward, her gaze landing on him in the shadows. An inexplicable look of relief crossed her face and she walked towards him, her hand extended.

He'd been ready to leave for the past half hour, but the sisters had kept him talking, their polite manners making his exit impossible. Now he was tempted to stride out of the room without excusing his poor behavior.

"Hello," Beth said. "I apologize. I didn't see you after the glare of the sun from outside. I'm sorry I kept you waiting."

She stopped as he shook her hand, her face flushed and her eyes widened in surprise.

He wished his reaction had been that simple. At least he hoped he hid the surge of desire that hit him, the approval he felt as he realized her hands were callused, hard, the sign of a worker.

"I wanted to talk to you about training me to be a barrel racer," she said. She hooked her thumbs in the back pockets of her jeans. One light brown eyebrow slid up. "I understand you're the best."

He recognized a challenge when he heard one. He tightened his features, hoping for impassiveness. "Yeah. The best."

"Well, you certainly don't lack in self-confidence," she chided, her chin rising slightly even as she smiled.

He kept his answer succinct. After all, he wasn't being hired for conversation. "Nope."

"I assume you have references. I've read some interviews, but I haven't heard who you've worked with lately."

"I trained two of the last three world champions. You can call Sherry Duncan and Lisa McDonald," he said, naming his two latest pupils. He wasn't used to having his credentials questioned, but he didn't blame the young woman for asking. No, that wasn't the problem.

But there was a problem. Or maybe several.

"Look, Miss Kennedy, I think there's been a mistake," he said, avoiding her gaze. "I'll be on my way."

"Wait!" He heard Beth call as he turned his back on her, not bothering to shake hands with her. He didn't want to touch her again. The last time had unsettled him for some strange reason.

"Where are you going?" she asked.

"On down the road. I have others interested in my services."

"I haven't said I'm not interested," she reminded him.

"You're not the only one to make the decision, lady. I don't work where I'm not wanted." He opened the door and walked out to his beat-up pickup, ignoring the whispering going on between the sisters.

Hearing footsteps behind him, he hoped it was Abby, the sensible older sister. But the tingling on the nape of his neck told him it was Beth.

Soft name. Feminine. Trouble.

"Mr. Davis, could we talk a minute?"

"Nothing to talk about," he muttered. All his instincts were yelling for him to get the hell out of there before she persuaded him to stay.

He slid behind the wheel and closed the door, but the window was down, since it was October, and she put her hand on the opening.

"What's your hurry?"

"I've been waiting over an hour for you to get your rear in gear, lady. I don't like to waste time." He kept staring straight ahead. He'd already noted her hazel eyes, the dash of freckles across her nose, the full lips that started a hunger in him that was dangerous.

Hell, she was too young for him to be thinking those thoughts. He was only thirty-two but he felt years older in comparison to her fresh beauty.

"I didn't have a flat tire on purpose."

"Doesn't take that long to fix a flat tire. Unless you're sitting helpless-like alongside the road waiting for Prince Charming." He figured even then someone would happen along pretty quick for a woman like Beth Kennedy.

She flushed and looked away. "I didn't have a spare," she muttered.

"What did you do?"

"I had to walk to a neighbor's house and call the garage in town and have them bring one out to me." Now she looked him in the eye. "I should've called here to warn you I'd be late. I apologize."

"No problem," he said, and cranked the engine in his truck.

"So I apologized. Why are you leaving?"

"I don't work with anyone who won't give one hundred percent."

Both of those pretty brows rose, almost disappearing in her soft bangs. "Who said I wouldn't?"

"You have to be hungry to make it in rodeo. You're not hungry."

"Oh, yes I am."

"How could you be? Your next meal doesn't depend on how well you race."

She studied him, which made him all the more uneasy. He knew some women were attracted to him. He'd had too many offers to deny the truth of it. But he was untrained in social skills.

"Does your next meal depend on your job?" she

asked casually. But he saw the intelligence in her eyes. More trouble.

He shrugged. "Not my next one, but eventually I'd run out. It did once."

"Mine did once, too. Not now, as you've obviously heard. But it's not food that drives me. And I think it's not food that drives you. That doesn't make me any less hungry. Does it you?"

Damn, why didn't she back off? He couldn't be anything but honest. "Nope."

"So, we have something in common."

"I charge a hefty fee." He was searching for reasons to leave. He should have known money wouldn't be one of them. But he'd try. He doubled his fee, watching her face as he named it.

"My, my, you are proud of your work, aren't you?"

The urge to justify that amount, to tell her just how good he was, surged through him, but he held it in check. "Yeah."

"Okay."

He stared at her, not sure what her single word meant. And irritated that she could be even more succinct than he was.

"Okay, what?"

"I'm agreeing to your price. I'm assuming that's in addition to room and board. Anything else?"

"Yeah. If I take on any other training jobs, I'll need stable space for the animals. I'll pay for the extra feed, of course."

"I'll have to check with Abby on that. She runs

the ranch. But I think it'll be okay. When can you start?''

What the hell was he doing? He'd had every intention of driving down that long, dusty driveway and never looking back. Now he was practically moved in.

"Wait a minute. I haven't seen you ride."

"So we'll try it for a week or two and then reevaluate. If you don't think I'm worth your time, you move on. Or if I don't like the way you work, you move on. If we're both satisfied, we keep going." She was watching him closely. When he didn't respond, she repeated her earlier question. "When can you start?"

"Uh, in the morning?"

"Right. It'll take about an hour to fix up a room in the bunkhouse. You'll take your meals at the house with us. The stable has a couple of empty stalls," she said, gesturing to the two-horse trailer he had hitched to his truck. "Want some help settling your horses?"

"No! I handle my animals. No one else touches them. Got that?"

"Got it. And I hope you take lots of sugar in your coffee," she returned.

He knew he was going to regret asking, but he couldn't help himself. "Why?"

"'Cause you need to sweeten up. Otherwise, everything around you is going to go sour," she snapped, stepping back from the truck.

"Maybe I need something more than sugar," he

retorted, determined to make her back down. "What do you say to that?"

"That you're out of luck unless you want to visit town and fork over some cash. That's none of my business as long as you do your job." Her chin was rising again, a sign he'd already figured out meant she was digging in her toes.

"I'll do my job, lady. You just see if you can stand the pace." He glared at her, but she said nothing else, simply giving him a careless salute and walking toward the house.

He watched the sway of her rear in those tight jeans and was afraid he might drool. Visiting town for some female companionship might be a necessity if he hung around Beth Kennedy for any period of time.

Damn, he'd gotten himself into a mess.

Beth could feel his glare on her. She hoped her trembling legs didn't show beneath her jeans. What had she gotten herself into?

She wanted to be a barrel racer. The best barrel racer in the world. She'd heard of Jedadiah Davis, read about him. She couldn't wait to have met him.

Of course, she should have called, but she'd thought she could get home quicker than she had. And she hadn't wanted to tell her sisters what she was up to.

She should have known he'd be offended by his wait. He was so full of himself—okay, so maybe he had a right to be self-confident. He *was* the best.

And the handsomest.

She hadn't expected his rugged good looks. Those piercing blue eyes seemed to read every thought in her head. But that must not be true, or he would have known he'd rocked her almost from the beginning.

Abby was anxiously waiting when she reached the house, taking Beth's thoughts away from her reaction to the man.

"Well? Are you going to train with Mr. Davis?"

"He's staying. I've got to clean out one of the unused rooms in the bunkhouse."

"I'll help," Melissa, the middle Kennedy sister, said from the doorway. "I've been intending to work on those rooms anyway." Since their visit to the lawyer's office a month ago, after their Aunt Beulah's death, learning of their inheritance, Melissa had been redoing the house, making it more efficient and more beautiful.

"Thanks, Missy," Beth returned, using her childhood name for Melissa. "Do you have time?"

"Yeah. Dinner's already in the oven for tonight, and I baked a cake this morning."

"Once he has one of your meals, Mr. Davis will never leave," Abby teased. "Did you negotiate a fee?" she asked her youngest sister.

"Yeah, and it's a good thing I inherited a lot of money." She told Abby the fee he demanded. "That's twice what I heard he charges, but he's well worth it. He probably doubled it because he doesn't think I have any talent," Beth muttered. "Or because he didn't like me."

"Why wouldn't he like you?" Melissa demanded to know, her hands on her hips. She was always the first to defend her sisters.

Abby chuckled. "Probably because she's hard-headed and demanding, Melissa."

"She's determined," Melissa corrected, "and charming."

Both her sisters almost doubled over in laughter.

"I swear, Missy, you'd say the Grinch was mis-understood," Beth said, hugging her sister.

"And she'd convince the rest of us," Abby added.

"Oh, you two," Melissa protested. "But I'm glad the man's going to take you on. He really is the best."

"Yeah, I know," Beth agreed. "Thank you both for letting me try this. I know it'll make us a little shorthanded on the ranch."

"We'll manage," Abby assured her. When they discovered their inheritance, all three had vowed to pursue their dreams, but actually doing so wasn't easy. "But why did a flat take so long?"

"I didn't get the spare fixed six months ago when I had the last flat."

"Aunt Beulah always said you should pay atten-tion to details," Abby reminded her.

"Yeah," Beth agreed with a sigh. "I think Jed Davis will be saying the same thing."

Beth gathered up clean sheets, a broom, a mop and bucket, and lots of cleaning supplies. Melissa fol-lowed her with a pillow, blanket and a set of towels.

Only two men occupied the bunkhouse right now, though Abby was looking for new hands.

Barney had been on the ranch long before the girls had come to live there when their parents died fifteen years ago. He'd had a casual male influence on their lives, but mostly, he'd been a friend. Beth had learned from Barney to whittle in rare moments of leisure. She trusted him.

The other cowhand, Dirk, kept to himself. He'd been on the ranch a little over two years, but he had forty years' experience on the range. He might not be overly friendly, but he worked hard.

Now Jedadiah Davis would become a part of their lives. As she made the bed, Beth couldn't help wondering if he'd stay long enough to get to know them, or move on, still a stranger.

A shiver passed through her. Something about the man bothered her. She believed his reputation, so there were no doubts there. But when he'd shaken her hand, she'd wanted to snatch it back, to retreat.

One look into his piercing blue eyes and she'd felt exposed, unable to hide. And then there was his response to her comments about sugar.

She hoped the man didn't think there were any extracurricular benefits to training her. *You wish,* her inner voice taunted.

Grinning ruefully, she admitted he was attractive. Her social life, in the face of Beulah's need of their help, had suffered. She didn't know much about men in that area. Her one attempt to gain some experience had been a disaster.

Fortunately, the man had moved on, leaving her at home to lick her wounds, never having to see him again. She sure wouldn't want to ruin her training with any...messiness.

"I can do that."

The deep burr of a voice didn't need identifying. She snapped straight up from her bent position over his bed. Spinning around, she put her hands on her hips, hoping to looked composed.

"No problem. We've just finished. That is, Melissa helped me, but she went back to the house to check on dinner." She scooped the towels up from the one chair in the little room. "Here's a set of towels. Toss the dirty ones over in that laundry basket. We pick up the dirty clothes every couple of days and return them washed the next day."

"I'll take care of my own laundry," he growled.

"Suit yourself, but if you're picturing me bent over a washtub, don't. We have good equipment and share the work." She didn't add that the new washing machine and dryer had arrived only a couple of weeks ago.

He nodded but said nothing else, just staring at her.

"Well, dinner will be at six. The other two men are Barney and Dirk. Introduce yourself and I'll see you at dinner."

"Did you ask Abby about my training other horses?"

She was glad she'd remembered to ask. They had plenty of space for the man to train horses. In fact, she hoped she might learn something about it. "Yes. She said that's not a problem."

"Good."

He continued to stare at her, not moving out of the doorway. Something warned her not to push past him. It was as if sparks would fly if she touched him.

"Need anything else?" she asked.

"No, I guess not."

"Then, welcome to the Circle K. Hope you like it here." She took a step forward. Still he didn't move.

Her mop, broom and pail were against the wall by the door. She moved to pick them up.

His big hand circled the broom and mop. "Want me to carry these to the house?"

Startled by his offer, she looked into his eyes. Beautiful blue eyes. "No, of course not. I'm no debutante, unable to do for myself."

Her aunt had worked them hard because it had been necessary. Or at least, they'd thought it had. And taught them a lot. But she'd done more than that. She'd given them a home together when Social Services had intended to separate them into three foster homes. She was their uncle's widow, no blood kin, but she'd taken them anyway.

"We'll see what you're made of tomorrow morning," he warned, as if he didn't believe her words.

But Beth wasn't about to show any fear. "You bet you will, cowboy."

Chapter Two

In spite of her brave words, Beth didn't sleep well that night.

After a meal where her stomach rolled every time Jed spoke, which, fortunately, wasn't often, she'd maintained her ground until the man had left the house. Then she'd hidden in her room, poring over the books she'd found on barrel racing. And any information she could find about Jedadiah Davis.

There was little written on Jed's early years. He'd made his mark on the rodeo circuit as a roper. Twice he'd won the national championship. Three other times he'd been in the top five. Then he'd hurt his arm in an auto accident and had turned to training.

And never looked back.

For the past four years, he'd been the man in demand. All the reports said he was a stern taskmaster. But he got results.

If he believed in his pupil.

One moment she was holding her breath, hoping he'd believe in her. The next moment she'd find herself pleading he'd move on down the road, leaving her to find another trainer.

He made her nervous.

When she reached the breakfast table, Abby offered her the entire morning off from ranch work, so she could have plenty of time to give to her training. But Beth couldn't be so selfish. She knew Abby was already shorthanded with Melissa working in the house all day.

"I haven't set up a specific time with Jed, yet. I thought I'd put in three or four hours, then head back to the house. After lunch, I can ride out with you again."

"That won't be enough time for you to get much done," Abby protested.

"Until you find another hand, Abby, I'm going to help."

Abby sighed. "I admit it would make things easier. Even though we finished the roundup, we had to neglect the fences, and we've got to bale the hay, and I'd like to move the larger herd to the south pasture."

"All in one day?" Melissa teased from the stove.

"If it's possible," Abby agreed with a grin.

"Seriously, I can ride out if it'll help," Melissa offered.

Abby and Beth exchanged grins. Though the two

of them had taken to the saddle, Melissa, while able to ride, preferred to spend her time in the kitchen.

"We won't ask for that much sacrifice," Abby assured her sister. "Someone will come along looking for a job any day now. You just keep feeding us."

"Yeah, last night's dinner was terrific," Beth added.

"How would you know?" Melissa returned. "You scarcely ate anything." Before Beth could come up with excuses, Melissa said, "Ring the bell for the guys."

Beth stepped to the back porch and banged on the triangle that hung from one rafter. Before the ringing had even stopped, three men emerged from the bunkhouse.

She didn't have any difficulty picking out Jed Davis. His broad-shouldered, narrow-hipped figure topped the other two men by three or four inches. Drawing a deep breath, she waited for them to reach her.

As she'd expected, Jed let the other two go first. Before he could move past her with a nod, she touched his arm. He came to an abrupt halt, his gaze settling on her hand.

She jerked it back.

"Yeah?" he asked warily.

Her prepared speech flew out of her head. "Is it all right if we start about ten?"

"Ten? Is that your idea of an early start?"

The scorn in his voice flailed her—and made her

so mad she wouldn't have explained if he'd begged her. Taking on a drawl she'd heard other women affect, she replied, "That's right, sugar. I need to get my nails done before I can get on a horse."

Then she sashayed in front of him into the house.

She figured he'd be packed and gone before noon. And good riddance to him. When she didn't hear footsteps behind her right away, she wondered if he'd even come in for breakfast.

"Where's—" Abby began, but the sound of the back door opening again stopped her question. "There you are, Jed. I thought maybe you'd gotten lost."

"No, ma'am."

Melissa set a platter of scrambled eggs on the table where sausage and bacon already awaited eager hands. Then she pulled two pans of biscuits out of the oven.

Beth picked up the coffeepot and began filling cups, while Abby poured glasses of orange juice. As she carried the glasses to the table, Abby addressed Jed.

"I'm sure Beth explained about the late start this morning. I'm hoping we'll find more men right away, but Beth is still willing to help out before she starts training."

"Help out with what?" he asked, ignoring the plate of eggs Barney was offering him.

Everyone in the kitchen, except Beth, seemed surprised by his question. Abby, after shooting a look at Beth, said, "Whatever needs to be done. We work with Dirk and Barney, like anyone on a ranch."

"All three of you?"

Melissa's cheeks flushed. "Not me. I used to help some days, but I prefer the cooking and housework."

Beth added, "We always felt meals like Melissa turns out are fair trade."

Both hands, seated at the table, stuffing their faces, made grunts of approval.

"I can see why. Your cooking is the best, Miss Melissa." Jed sent Melissa a smile that had Beth's insides quivering with jealousy.

He turned to Abby. "I understand that there's work that has to be done. How can I help?"

"Oh, no!" Abby protested. "Your time's too valuable for—I mean, Beth didn't hire you to do ranch work. We'll manage."

"I'll help," he said decisively, as if it was his decision. "Then maybe I'll get an extra hour with my pupil, if she can work it in."

There was a little sarcasm in those last words, Beth realized. Maybe she deserved it, since she'd given him a smart answer earlier. But he'd made her mad.

His blue gaze settled on her face, as if he expected her to comment.

She took a bite of eggs and chewed as though her life depended on it.

Abby, after looking at her, too, said, "I'm sure we can work that out."

Okay, so he'd jumped to an erroneous conclusion. That didn't mean the lady had to gull him with her response about a manicure. Jed studied her hands from under his lashes as he ate the fine breakfast Melissa Kennedy had prepared.

Beth's nails were short, clean and unpolished. Working hands, as he'd earlier noted. And sexier than any of the red claws he'd seen on women who thought they were all dolled up. But that smart mouth of hers was going to cause trouble.

When he got up from the breakfast table, he carried his dishes to the sink. The other two men stared at him, then hurriedly did the same thing. Melissa rewarded them all with a grateful smile.

"Where do you want me, Miss Abby?" he asked, awaiting instructions from the lady boss.

"Are you any good at fence repairs?" she asked.

With a lopsided grin, he said, "I've ridden more fence lines than you can imagine."

"Great. Why don't you and Beth ride—"

"No!" Beth shrieked.

"No!" Jed said, quieter but just as determined. When Abby stared at him, he added, "I don't need any help."

"It will go faster with the two of you, and it will give you a chance to get to know each other. You can finish the fence on the south pasture by mid-morning, before Barney and Dirk get the herd over there."

"You can't start baling hay by yourself," Beth protested. "What if something happens?"

"I'll take the new cell phone. But I've done it

before. It's a boring job, but safe.'' Abby stood and stared at the rest of the room. "It's settled. I'll see all of you at lunch.'' She turned and walked out of the kitchen.

Barney and Dirk shuffled out the back door. Jed stared at Beth. When she still sat at the table, her lips pressed tightly together, he prodded, "Are you waiting for your manicure? Or are you going to lead the way to the south pasture?''

"Manicure?'' Melissa questioned.

"He's teasing me, Missy. Don't worry about it." Beth stood and glared at him. "You got gloves?''

"Yeah. They're at the bunkhouse.''

"Go get them and I'll meet you at the barn.''

Beth breathed a sigh of relief when Jed left the house.

"Are you sure the two of you are going to get along?'' Melissa asked.

"No.'' Beth tried to paste a smile on her face, knowing her single answer reeked of despair. "I can't seem to help putting up his back, Missy. I don't intend to, but he made me so mad—''

"When?''

"Out on the porch, before breakfast. I was going to explain, truly, but I blurted out that we'd start at ten and he assumed I was going to go back to bed or something. So I told him we couldn't start earlier because I had to get a manicure.''

Melissa laughed. "You've never had a manicure.

I tried to paint your nails once, and you screamed as if I were torturing you.''

''Do you think you have to remind me? It was a silly answer, but it was the most decadent thing I could think of.''

''Well,'' Melissa began, putting an arm around Beth's shoulders, ''I think you might need to do some fence-mending of your own, in addition to the real fences, while you're out there with him this morning.''

''Yeah,'' Beth agreed glumly, and went to fetch her hat and gloves.

Outside the barn, she selected two horses, one a sturdy, rawboned roan that could easily carry Jed's big body. For herself, she chose a part Appaloosa mare she'd named Snowdrop. After putting bridles on them, she tied them to the corral fence and went into the barn to fetch the rest of the gear.

Much to her surprise, she almost ran into Jed in the shadowy interior. He was saddling one of his horses.

''You don't need to ride him. I've got a horse in the corral for you.''

''I always ride my own horses.'' His no-nonsense response irritated her again.

Taking a deep breath, she said calmly, ''It's your choice. Me, I wouldn't work my horse after traveling with him, unless I had to.''

Without waiting for a response, she moved on to the tack room. Lifting down her saddle and the blanket that went with it, she turned around to discover Jed standing in the doorway.

"You've got a point," he said, though she heard the reluctance in his voice. "Okay if I use my own gear?"

"Of course." She wasn't about to let him see that she enjoyed his capitulation. He followed her back into the autumn sunshine and she indicated the roan.

"That's Buster. He's no racehorse, but he has a steady gait and he's dependable."

"Thanks."

After throwing the blanket on Snowdrop, she put the saddle in place, then began buckling and cinching.

"You do that like you were born to it," Jed offered after watching her.

"I was nine when we came here to live. Aunt Beulah didn't waste any time teaching us about ranch life. And she didn't suffer fools gladly."

"Glad to hear it," Jed returned, saddling Buster.

Beth almost burst into laughter. If he'd tried, he couldn't have come closer to the dry retorts that had punctuated Beulah's long silences.

It had taken the girls several years to realize what a softy Beulah was beneath that stern exterior. But she wasn't one to wear her feelings on her sleeve. And she didn't believe in spoiling children. They received practical gifts on their birthdays. And warm hugs.

That same behavior was repeated at Christmas. Though she wasn't effusive, Beulah made them feel welcome. She fed them, clothed them, and made sure they attended school. And most important of all, she made it possible for them to stay together.

So Beth gave no response to Jed's comment, other than to give him a sunny smile that seemed to surprise him. And that surprise alone was enough to keep her cheerful for a while.

They'd been riding for an hour. Not in companionable silence, but at least they hadn't had an argument. Finally Jed decided he should make use of their time together.

"Tell me why you want to barrel race."

She seemed startled by his question.

He waited, giving her a few minutes to pull herself together.

"It's the main event open to women."

"Others are opening up. There's a small circuit only for cowgirls here in Texas."

She nodded. "When I first thought of it, I wanted to ride because of the money. It seemed we never had enough. Melissa was dreaming of a dishwasher. Abby talked about wanting to increase our irrigation system. Aunt Beulah didn't ever indulge herself. I wanted—I wanted a lot of things." With a sigh, she sent him another smile. "I saw myself in the role of triumphant savior."

"And now?"

"Now, Aunt Beulah is dead, and, much to our surprise, the three of us have a lot of money. Aunt Beulah had put away oil money from earlier years that we didn't know about. But I want to prove myself, to be the best at something. Melissa, well, you've eaten her cooking. She's a natural-born nester, willing to mother the world. And Abby, she's an expert on ranching. After working hard all day, she spends her evening reading the ranching magazines, even textbooks on grazing, breeding.''

He didn't want to hear this. He'd be a lot better off if he could keep believing she was weak, lazy, selfish, vain. All those things he'd assumed before he'd met her.

All those things she'd disproved every minute he spent with her. She was beautiful, but seemed unaware of it. A hard worker, but took it for granted. Concerned for her sisters, but seemed not to worry about herself.

"So you decided to take up barrel racing?"

She sent him an impish grin that had his heart beating faster. Didn't she know how much he was affected by her lips? Or her tight body, moving with the rhythm of her horse?

"Well, I happen to like riding fast.''

"And winning?''

"That, too,'' she added, her smile widening.

"And satin shirts?''

"If I admit to that, are you going to condemn me?'' she asked, her expression now wary.

He looked away as he shook his head no.

"You see, Beulah didn't think clothes were very important. And I was the youngest, so I never got anything new. Abby and Melissa wore them first.''

Then she shook her head. "That's not true. Occasionally, they were too hard on the clothes and they'd be worn out by the time Melissa had finished with them. I'll never forget the one time I got a new pair of jeans." This time she beamed at him, and he groaned under his breath. He had to stop hearing these confidences before he swept her into his arms and promised her anything her heart desired.

A peal of laughter surprised him. He looked at her again.

"I was so proud of my new jeans, I insisted on wearing them while we were riding fence line. And I ripped one leg into shreds on a barbed wire fence."

"Why was that so funny?"

She chuckled again. "Oh, it's hard to explain. I was afraid to face Aunt Beulah, but she just told me to take them off, and she spent the rest of the evening sewing them up again."

"She sounds like a fine lady," he said, still not understanding her laughter.

"Sometimes you remind me of her."

Her quiet words startled him more than her laughter. "What do you mean? I can't sew a lick."

She laughed again. "I didn't figure you could."

He glared at her, his only defense, and kicked Buster in the sides to speed up. They'd only found one break so far. No sense in wasting time talking.

They finished the south fence line in a little over three hours. Jed was nothing if not efficient. He'd started out trying to keep Beth from helping.

She ignored his tactics and pitched in.

By the third break, he still barked orders, but he included her in the work. When she'd said he reminded her of Aunt Beulah, she'd meant his gruff exterior, but she already suspected underneath was a man with a heart of gold.

When they reached the corral, he took care of his own horse, leaving her to deal with Snowdrop. Just the way she wanted it.

"What horse are you planning to train?" he asked, his back to her.

"I don't know."

He turned to frown at her. "You don't know?"

"I thought it would be best to wait until I found a trainer and got his opinion about a horse. I love Snowdrop, but she doesn't have the speed I'll need."

He just stared at her.

"Any suggestions? Do you know of a good horse? Price isn't a problem."

"Damn, woman, you're giving me carte blanche to rip you off. Don't do that." He turned his back to her again.

She grinned. Did he think she was no judge of men? She might not know how to handle a man romantically, but she'd learned from Aunt Beulah how to judge a man's character. And even if he didn't like her, Jed Davis was a man to be trusted.

"So you want me to pick a horse on my own?"

He'd just reached up to lift the saddle off Buster, but instead, he rested his hands on the saddle and bowed his head until his Stetson was almost resting on the leather. Then he gave a gusty sigh, as if she was too much to bear.

"There's this pretty little sorrel on the next ranch. We'd look good together, but I don't think she has the cutting ability we'd need. Or Bill Garland has several horses he's been trying to sell me," she continued, wondering how long he'd maintain his silence. "Of course, Aunt Beulah wouldn't ever buy a horse from him. She called him a shyster."

"I know a horse." His terse words stopped her.

"You do?"

"About an hour's drive from here, just into the Oklahoma panhandle. It'll cost you a pretty penny."

"Okay."

He dragged his saddle and blanket off Buster and stalked into the stable. She took her saddle and followed him.

"So, when can we go see him?"

"I'll go pick him up. I can get a better price without you there." He never looked at her.

"No."

"Yes."

"No. I won't agree to the purchase unless I get to see the animal first."

"The minute Joe knows the horse is for you, the price will be over the moon. You'll just have to trust me on this. I'm going alone."

"No."

Jed dumped his saddle on the stable wall where one of his horses was penned. Then he turned around to stare at her, his hands riding his hips and a fierce look on his face. "Lady, when I train someone, *I'm* in charge. I make the decisions."

"Mister, when *I'm* buying a horse, I get to take a look before I put down my money." She put her hands on her hips and glared back.

"I knew this wasn't going to work," he muttered. "I'll pack up and be out of here in an hour."

He turned his back again and Beth felt her heartbeat racing. She didn't want him to go. Because he would be a good teacher, she assured herself. That was the reason.

"Boy, you sure give up easy. It's a wonder you were successful at all on the rodeo circuit."

When he spun around and began advancing on her, Beth didn't hesitate to beat a retreat. Until her back hit the stable door across the aisle and she had nowhere to go.

That didn't stop Jed Davis from coming after her.

Chapter Three

Jed couldn't believe the woman. She was driving him crazy, with her big eyes, sweet lips and sassy mouth. But starting now, he was going to let her know who was boss. He wouldn't be taking her with him to Oklahoma.

Putting his hands on each side of her, trapping her against the stable door, he said firmly, "Don't you ever dare call me a quitter again."

"I don't guess I'll need to if you don't quit." She sounded real sure of herself, but Jed knew he was making her nervous, because she stuck her trembling fingers into her jean pockets.

"I ought to quit," he muttered, staring into her eyes, fighting the urge to kiss her until she agreed to whatever he wanted.

"But you're not going to?" Her hopeful look reminded him of a puppy that had followed him home a long time ago.

"I guess not. But I'm going to buy this horse without you." At least he could stand his ground there.

"That's not fair, Jed. If I'm going to work with the horse, I have to see him first. We might not get along."

"I wouldn't choose a horse you couldn't work with." He might not know a lot of things, but he knew horses.

"I don't see why I can't go," she continued to argue.

"I'm telling you, Joe will triple the price once he knows who wants it."

"How will he know?"

Jed frowned at her. "What do you mean?"

"Well, are you going to introduce me as Beth Kennedy, wealthy woman, looking to be parted from her money?" She gave him a winsome smile, as if she'd made a joke.

"Hell, no. Why would I do that?"

"Then how will he know who I am?"

Figuring he was losing his mind, hanging this close to Beth, smelling her, wanting to touch her, he suddenly backed away, releasing her from his improvised jail. "He'll know you're the one I'm buying the horse for."

"So? I don't go around in jewels and a tiara. He won't know I have money."

"He'll know when he sees your check." Word

always got around when there was a chicken to be plucked.

"You write a check and then I'll write you a check later. We could do that, couldn't we? Oh!" She beamed at him and he held his breath. "I know. We'll tell him I'm your girlfriend!"

Jed thought he was going to choke to death. He coughed several times to regain his breath, and Beth beat him on the back.

"Are you all right? What's wrong?" she asked, her eyes wide with concern.

"Damn, woman! That's the craziest idea I've ever heard." He backed up a couple of more steps. This time *she* came after *him*.

"Why?"

"Joe would never believe it."

"You think I'm not pretty enough?"

Jed slumped against the opposite stable door, defeat filling him. He couldn't lie to her. "You're too pretty. Joe wouldn't believe anyone like you would be interested in someone like me."

Her eyelids lowered and she stepped to his side, one hand sliding up his chest. "Sure he would, sugar. I'm a good actress." She was using the drawl that had fooled him this morning when she'd mentioned that blasted manicure.

He had to do something to get her away from him before he wrapped his arms around her and looked for the nearest pile of hay. "Okay, you can go. Ask Miss Abby if she needs us after lunch."

Excitement filled her. But before she raced to the

house to do as he said, she stretched herself against him and kissed his cheek. "Thanks, Jed."

Then she was gone.

"Lord have mercy, what have I gotten myself into?" he asked the horses in the barn.

None of them answered.

Already realizing Jed preferred silence to conversation, Beth tried to contain herself on the ride into Oklahoma and not ask any questions. That resolve lasted for almost half an hour. Then her excitement took over.

"How'd you learn about this horse?"

"I trained him."

"For barrel racing?"

"No, as a cutting horse."

He stared straight ahead at the road, never looking at her.

"How do you know he'll make a good racer?"

"He's fast."

"Did you—"

"Do you ever stop asking questions?" He turned to glance at her, irritation on his face.

She grinned, refusing to be offended. "Nope."

"Listen, he's got strong haunches, he's low to the ground, but he's got a long stride, and he's very intelligent."

"Why didn't you buy him? He sounds perfect. Was he too pricey?"

"Nope. He's too small for a man my size. That's why I think Joe will sell him. Joe's a big man, too."

She let her gaze wander his length, from the Stetson, past his broad shoulders to his long, hard thighs, down to his dusty boots. She drew a deep breath. She didn't know how much more testosterone she could handle.

"He doesn't have a wife to ride her?"

"Nope. He's a widower, no children. He breeds quarter horses. Shorty doesn't fit the mold, so Joe didn't want him for breeding stock. He's a gelding."

She thought about what he said. "Then we ought to get him cheap."

"He's got good bloodlines."

"But—"

"We'll pay a good price, but it will be a fair one. Just don't give away that you're the real buyer."

His clipped order wasn't anything new, but it made Beth want to have him experience some of the discomfort she felt at his curt tone. Abby had pointed out to her more than once that her responses weren't always wise ones.

"Then I'd better practice being your girlfriend," she said as she undid her seat belt. Then she slid across the bench seat until her body was pressed against his right side.

He jerked the wheel in shock. "What the hell are you doing?" he snarled when he had the truck under control. "Get back to your side of the truck!"

"You're not being very friendly, Jed," she teased, glad to see he was capable of losing his iron control. "I won't be able to convince Joe unless I'm used to touching you.'' She lifted her left hand and settled it on his tense shoulder.

Apparently she'd gone too far. Jed yanked the wheel to the right as he stood on the brakes. Before Beth even realized his intent, he'd stopped on the side of the road.

Slamming the truck into Park, he reached for her without warning. His lips came down on hers, hard and demanding. Hot, controlling.

Beth, pressed against his chest, her breasts flattened, her eyes closed, resented his attempt to conquer. She knew that was all he intended. She even realized he wasn't going to hurt her. Just conquer her.

But she was made of sterner stuff than Jed Davis realized. And she gave as good as she got. Her hands slid up his chest to riffle through his dark hair. Her mouth moved under his.

And the kiss changed.

Suddenly they were equally involved in the touching, the demanding…the sizzle. So much so that Beth thought she was going to faint. But she was going to enjoy every second of it until then. Jed Davis was some kisser.

He almost threw her away from him only seconds later, staring at her as if she'd been a rattlesnake he'd found in his bed.

''Lady, you're crazy!'' he snapped, but she noted that his breathing was no more even than hers.

''Me? I'm not the one who grabbed—who started this.''

"You should've kept your seat belt on. Put it on now!" he ordered as he faced the front of the truck again, refusing to look at her.

This time she accepted his order. Sliding back across the bench seat, she snapped the seat belt and faced forward. If she looked at him, she was afraid she might beg for another kiss.

Jed breathed a sigh of relief when they reached Joseph Lander's ranch. He'd made a big mistake letting Beth come with him. In fact, he'd made a big mistake taking her on as a pupil.

He didn't mix business and pleasure. In fact, he didn't indulge in much pleasure. His goals were too important. And he never stayed in one place too long. He had learned early in life that if you stayed in one place too long, you began to care. And then it was just that much easier to get hurt when you were forced to move to a new foster home.

He wouldn't be staying long at the Circle K, that was for sure. Because the lady beside him had already shown him enough pleasure to scare the daylights out of him.

Not bothering to tell her to stay in the truck, because he knew she wouldn't, he got out and headed for the barn. He figured Joe wouldn't be in the house in the middle of the afternoon.

Before he got to the barn, however, the man he was looking for strode out to meet him. "Jed Davis! Good to see you, boy. How have you been?"

Jed shook his hand and returned the greeting. Before he'd finished, Joe's gaze went over his shoulder.

"Well, hello, there, little lady. You with this scalawag?" Joe asked with a grin.

Jed tried not to stiffen as Beth stepped to his side, sliding her arm through his. "Yes, I am," she said clearly, that beaming smile on her face.

"You're steppin' up in the world, Jed," Joe said with an approving nod.

"Thanks." Jed spent several more minutes passing the time of day with the rancher. Certain protocol had to be followed before he could get down to business. Finally he said, "I wondered if you still had Shorty?"

"Shorty? That scrub? Yeah, he's here." A thoughtful look came into Joe's eyes. "You interested in him?"

Jed shrugged, as if he wasn't sure. "I might be."

"What for? He's not big enough to carry you."

"Yeah, but I've got a smaller rider in mind. I think he might work."

"I'll show him to you, but I'm not sure I want to part with him." He turned toward the barn, then stopped. "Little lady, it's pretty dusty out there. You want to wait in the house? My housekeeper can fix you some iced tea."

Jed tensed, afraid Beth would blast the man between the eyes.

"Why, how thoughtful of you, but I don't like to let Jed out of my sights. Besides, I dressed cowboy so I'd fit in," she told the old man, blinking her lashes to great effect.

"Honey, I've never seen a cowboy look as good as you, but you're welcome to come along," Joe said, before turning again toward the barn.

Jed looked at Beth and she dared send him a wink along with her smile. He barely shook his head at her and went after Joe. She was wearing her jeans, but after lunch she'd changed to a soft rose-colored blouse and added some silver earrings. Joe was right about how good she looked.

And tasted.

Nope, he wasn't going to think about those moments in his truck. Because if he did, he'd go crazy.

On the other side of the barn, Joe hollered at one of the cowboys working in a nearby corral. "Larry, fetch Shorty out of the pasture."

Jed caught up with Joe and leaned against the corral, watching the action going on around him. Suddenly he saw someone he knew.

"Floyd? Is that you?"

An older cowboy, cleaning out the stables, straightened and squinted into the sun. "Jed?" He threw down the pitchfork he'd been wielding and came out of the barn to give Jed a hug. They'd worked together when Jed first went out on his own. Floyd had helped Jed learn a lot of lessons.

"How you doing, boy?" Floyd asked as he stepped back.

"Fine. And yourself?"

Floyd let his gaze slip to the boss and then back to Jed. "Just fine."

"Better get back to work, Floyd," Joe said, and all geniality was gone from his voice.

"Yes, sir," Floyd muttered. He sent a regretful look toward Jed and walked back into the barn.

Jed turned to look at Joe. "You unhappy with Floyd?"

Joe shrugged. "He's not a hard worker."

Beth moved closer to Jed and slipped her arm through his again. "He seemed nice," she said cheerfully, smiling at Joe.

Joe's mouth tightened. "He won't be staying here long. First excuse I can find, I'll send him down the road."

Jed frowned. He didn't know what had gone wrong between Joe and Floyd, but he knew who he'd trust first. And it wasn't Joe. He wished he had some time to speak to his old friend alone.

As if she'd read his mind, Beth moved over to the rancher and began asking him about two horses in a separate corral beside the barn. Joe, always playing the gallant, took her arm and led her over there.

Jed backed toward the barn, keeping his eye on Joe. When he reached the door of the barn, he leaned against it, casually, and called softly. "Floyd?"

"Yeah, boy?" Floyd responded just as softly.

"What's going on?"

"You mean with old moneybags?"

"Yeah."

"I caught him abusing a horse. He says I was trying to show him up. I've only been here about a month. Can't afford to blow off my job. But I reckon I'll have that decision made for me soon. Some of the other hands have been talkin'.''

Jed had heard rumors about Joe, but he'd never had proof. His jaw hardened. He knew Floyd would have trouble working for a man who abused his animals. As would Jed.

''Want a new job?''

''Yeah. You heard of any?''

''Yep. I'll guarantee you one. Got much to pack?''

''Nah. You know me. I travel light.''

''As soon as we finish business, go pack your things.''

He didn't want Floyd to upset Joe until his business was done. He saw the cowboy coming back across the pasture, a rope on Shorty.

Moving to the corral, he opened the gate and the cowboy led the horse inside. Jed then made sure the gate was closed and watched as the cowboy took his rope off Shorty. He studied the horse to see if he was okay.

Shorty was just as Jed remembered him. Short, compact, with good speed and cutting ability. He wasn't happy being penned up.

Joe came to Jed's side, along with Beth. ''He's kind of frisky, since he doesn't get ridden all that often. I had a small man who rode him, but he moved on. So no one's been on him in a while.

Jed shrugged, his gaze fixed on the horse.

''He looks so sweet,'' Beth said, her drawl in place

so she sounded as if she knew nothing about horses. "Will he bite me?" she asked as she tentatively put her hand through the railing.

"He might, honey. You'd best not try to pet him," Joe warned.

Jed didn't spare Beth a look. She could take care of herself. He'd already learned that. He concentrated on the horse.

"I'm interested, Joe. How much you want for him?"

Joe began the standard disclaimer, assuring Jed he didn't want to sell him. When Jed finally got him to name a sum, it was way too high. Negotiating the price down, he was about to accept the last offer, when Beth tugged on his arm.

"Sweetie, I don't think you should pay so much. That other one we looked at was much friendlier and he didn't cost so much."

Joe stiffened. "What other horse did you look at?"

Jed gave Beth a sideways look. She was proving to be quite an actress. "Well, I don't think I should—"

Joe was so eager he couldn't wait for Jed to finish. "Hell, Jed, you're a friend. I guess I can let you have Shorty for a little less. After all, you trained him." Then he knocked another two hundred off the price.

Jed couldn't let Beth's playacting down, so he appeared reluctant to take the horse. In the end, he bought him for four hundred less than he expected to pay.

Pulling his checkbook out of his hip pocket, he wrote a check for the final amount and handed it to Joe. "Thanks, Joe. Pleasure doing business with you."

"Anytime, Jed, anytime. Need some help loading him?"

Jed gave him a lopsided grin. "Nah, Beth will help me, won't you, darlin'?"

She grinned. "You bet. Where's that bridle we brought along?"

Jed had hung it on the corral. He took it and handed it to Beth. "Go softly. He's spooked."

"You're not gonna let her go in there, are you, Jed? She don't know nothing about horses," he warned.

But Jed knew, after riding with Beth all morning, that she knew a lot about horses. And he wanted to see how she and Shorty got along. He'd jump in if necessary.

Beth strode confidently into the corral, then slowed her pace. Hiding the bridle behind her back, she approached the uneasy horse, her soft voice crooning. "Hello, pretty boy. How are you? Glad to meet you. Come with me, now. We're going to take you home with us. You'll like it, I know. All you have to do is…"

Jed thought she could convince anyone or anything to accompany her with that silky, sexy tone. Even Joe seemed mesmerized by her talking.

Shorty didn't come to her, but he didn't run away, either. When she reached him, she rubbed his nose and stroked his neck before she slipped the bridle on him slick as could be.

"Damn! I thought she was a dude," Joe complained.

"Got another surprise for you," Jed said calmly as Beth was leading Shorty out of the corral.

Joe turned to him with a wary look. "What's that?"

"I'm going to take that unwanted cowboy off your hands. Floyd is going with me."

"You can't do that! He hasn't finished the three months I've paid for. He can't leave yet."

"Well, now, Joe, I believe you'd better just let him go. You're both unhappy. There's no reason to prolong the misery," he added, looking directly at Joe.

The old man seemed to read something in Jed's gaze that had him looking away. In a grim voice, he said, "Fine. Take him. I don't want him here."

Jed gave him a nod and walked to Beth's side. He took the bridle and gave her the keys to the horse trailer. "Go open up for me, sweetheart, okay?"

Her eyes widened at his endearment, but he figured he owed it to her for the "sweetie" she'd used earlier. Besides, it felt good.

By the time he was loading Shorty into the trailer, Floyd came racing out of the bunkhouse, a satchel in his hand. "Is the job still there?" he asked, breathless as he reached the truck.

Beth turned to stare at Jed.

"Sure is. Joe says it's okay for you to go. You

may owe him some money since he said he paid for three months.''

Floyd gave a grunt. ''He hasn't paid me at all. Told me I'd get paid at the end of three months, if I was satisfactory.''

''You want to go collect a month's pay?'' Jed asked.

''Nope. I don't want that man's money, if you're sure there's a job waiting for me.''

''Beth? Miss Abby said she was looking for help. I can vouch for Floyd. He's a good worker.'' He stared into Beth's hazel eyes, hoping she'd back him up.

After a long, steady look, she turned to Floyd and extended her hand. ''The Circle K can use a cowboy with that kind of a recommendation. As long as you have no trouble working for a woman.''

''No, ma'am, I don't. I don't have a horse right now. Do you have a ride or two for me?''

''You bet. What about gear?''

''I've got to get it from the barn. Then I'll be ready.''

While Floyd ran to the barn, Jed tied Shorty in place and stepped out of the trailer. ''Thanks, Beth. I appreciate your offering Floyd a job.''

''Abby will be grateful. And I'm grateful. Shorty looks good.''

Yeah, everything had worked out well. Jed let out a sigh, ready to hit the road before anything could go wrong.

But he realized he'd let his guard down too soon when, with the addition of Floyd in the cab of his truck, he found Beth pressed against his side for the entire ride home.

Chapter Four

By the time they reached the ranch, Jed's body was so tight he wasn't sure he could walk straight. Beth's lithesome form was imprinted on him. When she slid out of the truck, he felt as if part of him had been amputated.

"Want me to take Shorty out of the trailer?" Floyd asked.

Jed, still seated behind the steering wheel, frowned at his friend. "No. I want Beth to do it."

"But she's just a little girl," Floyd protested.

Jed couldn't hold back a wry grin as he saw Beth's face over his friend's shoulder. "Is he right, Beth?"

"Nope. Thanks, Floyd, but if I'm going to ride Shorty, I have to get him used to me." Then she disappeared from sight.

"*She's* going to ride Shorty?"

"Yeah. She's one of the famous Kennedy sisters,

and she's decided to become a barrel racer.'' The news about the three sisters' inheritance had already spread like wildfire through the ranching community.

"And you bought Shorty for a song?'' Floyd asked, a grin spreading over his face. "Hot dang it! I'm gonna be grinnin' about that for months. Serves Joe right.''

Jed grinned in return. "You're going to have more than that to grin about. Wait until you taste Miss Melissa's cooking. And working for Miss Abby will be a pleasure after Joe. Let's go introduce you.''

He actually found a reason to linger outside until he made sure Beth got Shorty out of the trailer with no difficulty. When she headed for the closest corral, he took his friend to the main house.

Jed knocked on the back door and Melissa called for him to come into the big kitchen.

"Is Miss Abby still out working?''

"Yes, she is. Did you get the horse?''

Why didn't her beautiful smile tie him in knots like Beth's did? He frowned, pondering his susceptibility to the youngest Kennedy.

"Was the price too high?'' Melissa questioned, stepping closer.

"Huh? Oh, no, we got the horse. Beth is putting him in the corral. Then she'll come in. Uh, I want to introduce an old friend, Floyd Jenkins.''

"Welcome to the ranch, Mr. Jenkins,'' Melissa said, still smiling.

Floyd nodded and smiled, but his gaze swung back to Jed.

Feeling uncharacteristically unsure of himself, Jed rubbed the back of his neck. "The fact is, Miss Melissa, I offered Floyd a job here."

Though Melissa's eyes widened in surprise, she said, "I'm sure Abby will be pleased, Jed."

Before he could answer, Beth stepped into the kitchen. "Did Jed tell you about Shorty?" she asked.

"Shorty? No, he said his name is Floyd," Melissa replied, staring at them all, confusion in her eyes.

"Shorty's my new horse," Beth told her, chuckling.

"Oh, sorry, Floyd, I mean, Mr. Jenkins," Melissa said.

"Floyd's fine, ma'am."

"Where can we find Abby?" Jed asked. He couldn't take much more close quarters with Beth. Not if he was going to keep his sanity.

"She's helping move the herd to the south pasture," Melissa said. "You know, the one you rode fence in this morning."

"Right. We'll ride out to talk to her about Floyd," Jed said, spinning on his boot heel, anxious to escape.

"I'll saddle up Shorty and ride with you," Beth said, already following him to the door.

"No! You should wait—"

"It'll give me a chance to get to know him."

She never stopped coming. He was beginning to realize she always went at full speed. Finally he shrugged his shoulders. At least she'd be on a horse and not pressed against his side.

"Fine. You got a horse for Floyd?"

"Are you going to ride one of your horses? 'Cause if you are, he can ride Buster."

"Good enough."

Beth spent her time keeping her eye on the horse she rode and the man she followed. Shorty seemed perfect for her. He had a smooth gait and quick reactions. Though frisky at first, he settled down quickly.

The man who'd chosen him seemed just as perfectly suited to the job as the horse. Jed Davis had an easy way about him...except when he dealt with Beth. With her sisters, he was calm, well mannered and smiling.

The minute he looked at her, she could see the tension build. With a smile at his squared shoulders, she ruefully admitted she had much the same reaction. Especially after that explosive kiss in his truck.

"Want to stretch out the kinks?" Jed called over his shoulder. Without waiting for a response to his question, he put his heels into his horse's sides and leaned low over the saddle.

She laughed out loud in delight as Shorty responded to her urging. Jed had been right. The horse was fast. For the first time since Jed Davis had entered her world, she put all her concerns behind her and let the wind blow away any problems.

When Jed called a halt to their unspoken race, Beth reined in beside him and shot him a radiant smile.

There was an answering glint in his blue eyes, but he immediately looked away.

"Jed, Shorty is wonderful. Thank you!"

"You paid for him. Thank yourself," he said shortly.

Floyd, who'd lagged behind, pulled up beside them. "Man, you two were really flying."

As irritated as Beth was with the handsome cowboy beside her, she wasn't going to be rude to Floyd. With a smile, she said, "Shorty's great, isn't he? Sorry Buster isn't faster."

"No problem. He's a good ride."

"Abby and the herd should be just over that next hill," she added, looking only at Floyd. Then, without waiting for Jed's lead, she urged Shorty forward at a more sedate pace.

Jed followed Beth's lead. After all, they weren't training right now, and it was her and her sisters' ranch.

Besides, she was mad at him.

No surprise. He was mad at himself. What was wrong with him? Every time he looked at the woman, hunger rose up in him. Anyone would think he was a love-starved teenager.

His gaze slipped to her hips as she sat her saddle. He immediately turned away, only to catch sight of Floyd watching him, a grin on his face. Hell! He was going to regret bringing Floyd here if his friend figured out what was going on in his head.

They topped the rise, sounds of the herd meeting

them even as they saw the movement across the small valley.

"Abby's riding drag," Beth said, pointing to the back of the herd.

"Big job for one person," Floyd muttered, watching the action.

"Yeah," Jed agreed. He'd noticed the Kennedy sisters did what had to be done. They didn't back off from a challenge. "Let's go make the introductions and see if she could use some help."

Abby heard them coming and pulled up, though her gaze scanned the herd, watching for any problems.

"Miss Abby," Jed said as he pulled up near her. "I brought a friend who could use a job. Floyd Jenkins. Thought maybe you could use him."

"Thanks, Jed. You recommend him?"

Jed nodded. Since he'd only met Abby yesterday, he didn't know if his recommendation would hold any weight. "Why don't you and Floyd talk while I take over drag."

"I've got a better idea. Floyd and I will do drag together and you and Beth range yourselves on each side of the herd. That would help Barney and Dirk more."

He nodded, then looked at Beth. "Right or left?"

"Left," she said, becoming almost as terse as him. At least they'd have a herd of steers between them.

As she gathered her reins, he added, "Remember, Shorty's a cutting horse."

She rolled her eyes and rode off.

He wanted to grab her and shake her. A rider not prepared for action would get a hell of a surprise when a cow left the herd. Shorty wouldn't wait for an invitation.

So, in addition to keeping his side of the herd in line, Jed watched Beth and her new horse. Of course, it hadn't taken long for him to realize she could handle Shorty.

But he kept his eyes on her anyway.

Barney, on Beth's side, rode ahead to open the gate to the south pasture. Some of the animals, seeing an opportunity, turned aside. Beth moved forward to discourage them and Jed saw Abby leave the back of the herd to fill in Beth's place.

Floyd waved to him, he guessed to let him know the interview was a success, before tending to his chore. Once the herd had been funneled through the gate, Barney closed it and turned to the other riders.

"Nice to have a little help. Thanks."

Abby introduced Floyd and informed all of them that he'd be working on the Circle K ranch now. "I think we might as well call it a day. By the time we get our horses rubbed down, it'll be supper time."

Barney fell in with Floyd, asking questions about his background. Dirk kept to himself. Abby joined Beth, and Jed could tell they were talking about Shorty. At least he'd made the right decision there.

But he wasn't sure about his decision to take on Beth.

The problem was, he couldn't come up with any reason *not* to train her. The money would be good.

She was an excellent rider. The rapport she'd already established with Shorty was evident.

And he already knew the Kennedy women were hard workers.

So why was he thinking about running?

Because he was scared.

Scared of being hurt. Which made him sound like a sissy, he scoffed. No one had ever called him weak. He'd learned the reality of being on his own early. Orphaned at seven when his mother died, and already abandoned by his father before he was born, Jed had gone through the social system of foster homes.

No one had cared.

They weren't mean to him. No beatings. Well, hardly ever. But no one really cared about him. No one ever offered him a home. Just a place to stay.

But not for long.

That's the way he lived his life now. But it wouldn't be that way in the future. He was putting aside every penny he could. Because he was going to buy himself a home. A place he never had to leave.

He knew horses. And cattle. He understood men. He'd been around a few ladies, too. What he didn't understand, would probably never understand, were families. He'd accepted the fact that he would go through life alone.

Which meant the attraction he felt for Beth Kennedy was just that. Attraction. Nothing more. There was no future, no little house with flowers, no baby beds filled with sweet-smelling babies. Lust, yeah.

But Beth Kennedy wouldn't understand the rules of a one-night stand.

And he wouldn't be so careless with his reputation.

So he'd train her to be the best barrel racer there was. Then he'd move on down the road. Alone. Looking for a place of his own.

He squared his shoulders. That's why he couldn't run. What he'd make on this job might make it possible for him to start looking for that home. A small ranch, where he could train animals. Riders, too, if they came to him.

He'd just have to harden his heart—not his heart, his body. Then he laughed. Wrong again. His body was already hard. He'd have to keep his mind on work. That's what he'd have to do.

Business. He'd think of Miss Beth Kennedy as one big bankroll, giving him the ticket to his dreams. When he looked at her, he'd see dollar signs, not a soft, curvy woman with bright eyes and a killer smile.

Yeah, right.

When Jed stepped into the kitchen that evening, Melissa handed him a stack of messages.

"You are most definitely in demand," she said with a smile.

"Sorry. Hope these calls didn't take up too much time," he said with a frown.

"No, of course not. But word has gotten around

that you're here, and a lot of our neighbors would like to take advantage of that.''

He nodded awkwardly. On the one hand, he was pleased to know his reputation was growing. On the other, he didn't want to take advantage of the ladies. They'd been gracious in their welcome.

"Is there a message from the Stallingses?" Beth asked, suspicion in her voice.

Jed raised an eyebrow. "I don't know any Stallings." He flipped through the messages, but before he could determine the answer, Melissa spoke.

"You know there is. Word has gotten around about you hiring Jed. You know Sissy is going to be frothing at the mouth," she assured her sister with a smile. "But it was her daddy who called, not Sissy."

Beth glowered at him, and Jed watched her. "Why would that upset you?"

Beth ducked her head, studying her dinner.

Abby gave him his answer. "Those two have competed for everything from spelling champion to Homecoming Queen since we moved here."

Jed couldn't imagine anyone having a chance against Beth, but he didn't comment on Abby's words.

"You won't train her, too, will you?" Beth demanded.

He considered her question, enjoying the anxiety that grew in her gaze. Then he relented. "It would be bad form to train competitors. Besides, I probably won't have time."

"Good." After that terse response, Beth turned her attention back to her meal.

After dinner, Abby offered the use of their phone for him to return his calls.

"Thank you, Miss Abby, but I've got a cell phone. I'll give the number to everyone so they won't be bothering Miss Melissa again." With a nod, he walked out with Floyd.

"You were right," Floyd said, scratching his stomach as they stepped off the porch.

"About what?"

"About Miss Melissa's cooking. And about working for Miss Abby. Smart lady."

"Yeah."

"And I haven't changed my mind about Miss Beth, either."

"What do you mean?"

"She's a cute little thing."

Jealousy surged through Jed. "Stay away from her, Floyd."

His friend seemed surprised. "I didn't mean anything. Hell, I'm old enough to be her father."

Jed nodded.

"But you're not."

He almost choked on the air he'd just breathed in. "Hey, Floyd, just quit thinking along those lines. I'm here to do a job. This is business, nothing else."

"Uh-huh," Floyd muttered, and opened the door to the bunkhouse.

After finishing cleaning the kitchen, Beth grabbed a couple of carrots and headed for the corral where she'd left Shorty. She needed to get the horse familiar with her.

Besides, she was too restless to stay inside.

After petting Shorty and giving him his treat, she talked to the animal, acquainting him with her voice. When she paused, however, she heard another voice.

A deep voice.

She couldn't see anyone, but she figured the sound was coming from the barn. What would Jed be doing in the barn at this time of night? Abby would never give him a chore this late unless it involved an emergency.

She moved quietly to the door of the barn and peered around it, as if she were sneaking up on someone.

Ridiculous. She wouldn't eavesdrop. Of course not. She'd been raised better than that. But she paused by the door anyway.

"How old is he?" Jed asked.

Since there was no one else around, Beth looked more closely at the cowboy and realized he was talking on his cellular phone. Why had he come to the barn to make his calls?

"Yeah, I can take him on. Should take about six weeks."

Six weeks? How long did he think it would take him to train her? She was hoping for more than six weeks.

"The price will include feed. I've made arrangements with the Kennedys. Yeah, bring him over tomorrow."

As Jed took the phone from his ear, he switched it to his left hand and used a pen he was holding to make some notes on a clipboard he had in his lap.

"Why are you calling from here?" she asked, stepping into the shadowy barn.

He jerked around, surprise on his face. "I didn't know you were there."

"I didn't know you were here, either, until I heard your voice. Won't your phone work in the bunkhouse?"

He tucked the phone into his shirt pocket and stood. "Yeah, but Barney came over to visit with Floyd. I didn't want to interfere with their social time."

"Floyd's bunking with you? There's room for you to have your own room."

To her surprise, Jed's cheeks heated up and he looked away. "It's better this way."

"Why?"

His jaw squared and he turned to stare at her. "Because I want him bunking with me, okay? My decision."

She held up both hands in surrender. "No problem."

Awkward silence filled the evening air.

"What are you doing out here at this time of night?" he suddenly asked, as if he were in charge.

He may have been hired to train her, but he was *not* her boss. "I don't think that's any of your business, unless I have a training curfew." It was only a little before eight, so she knew that couldn't be the case.

Not taking the bait, other than raising one eye-brow, he said, "We didn't talk about a schedule. Is seven too early a start for you?"

There was something in his look that told her he was remembering their encounter that morning. Too bad. She wasn't apologizing. "I think I can manage. How long will we work?"

He was about to answer when his phone rang.

"Your pocket is ringing," she pointed out.

With a growl, he pulled out the phone and answered it.

She could have moved back outside and given him some privacy, but she figured the call would be business, nothing personal.

"Yes, Mr. Stallings, I got your message."

She stiffened.

"I appreciate the offer, but I'm training Beth Kennedy for barrel racing. I don't think I should do the same for her competitor."

Jed paused for a moment, then said, "I suppose I could do that."

Beth's head jerked up and she stared intently at the man. Was he caving in? She'd have something to say about that, as much as she was paying.

"Why don't I come over tomorrow? There's no need to transport him if I don't think I can help."

As soon as he disconnected the phone, she stepped closer. "What are you offering to do for Mr. Stallings?"

He looked at her consideringly, and she frowned more fiercely. Then he drawled, "I don't think that's

any of your business unless it concerns your training.'' His remark sounded suspiciously like her response to his earlier question.

But she wasn't going to let him get away with that.
''I think it is, since Sissy Stallings is my biggest
competition.''

''Is she any good?''

''Yes. So it *is* my business.''

''Nope, it isn't. I'm going to look at a gelding her
dad wants trained as a cutter.''

''Oh.'' She couldn't complain about that. ''Was
that why he called in the first place?''

''Nope. He wanted me to help Sissy out, like you
suspected.''

There was a teasing glint in his eyes, a small smile
on his lips, that caught her attention. ''Thanks,'' she
muttered, wanting to turn away, to break their ac-
knowledgment of each other, but she couldn't.

''It's a rule I follow. Has nothing to do with you.''

What was he trying to do? Tell her he wasn't interested in her for anything but business? Well, neither was she! ''I didn't think it did.'' Then she remembered the question she'd asked earlier. ''How
long will we practice? I need to know so I can tell
Abby whether I can work tomorrow.''

''I'd like to put in a couple of hours in the morning
tomorrow. Then repeat it just before supper. I don't
want you practicing in between for a few days, until
Shorty gets used to the routine. And I don't want you
riding him for ranch work.''

She didn't like his bossiness, but she'd tolerate it. For now. "Okay."

"We'll work six days a week. Sundays you will be off. Any questions?"

"Saturday evening? You work then?"

"Yeah. Is that going to cut into your social life too much?"

There was the same sneer she'd heard in his voice on the porch that morning, the one that had driven her to respond with her remark about a manicure.

She should know better this time.

But not likely.

With that sugary drawl, she said, "No problem. My *friends* don't mind a late date." And she flounced out of the barn.

Chapter Five

Her words bothered him.

No matter how much he berated himself for his taunts, no matter how much he tried to dismiss her response, it bothered him. He told himself she probably didn't have late dates, like she didn't have manicures.

But he couldn't lie to himself.

The cowboys in this part of Texas would have to be blind and crazy not to come courting. Her beauty and independence alone would be more than enough to draw them. Add in wealth and a good ranch, and she could be as homely as a mangy dog and they'd flock to her door.

So he'd lain in his bed and listened to Floyd snore, trying to remind himself why he'd invited the man to bunk with him to begin with.

It was silly, really. But his reaction to Beth made

some safeguards necessary. He didn't want to have a readily available place where he could be alone with her.

"Yeah," he muttered with a quiet, cynical laugh. Like the wealthy, beautiful Miss Kennedy would condescend to visit the bunkhouse.

He immediately pictured her luscious form bent over his bunk, putting on the sheets. He'd have to give all three ladies credit. They didn't seem infatuated with their wealth.

They were all friendly.

They were all beautiful.

They were all wealthy.

They were all off-limits to him. Not that it mattered about Melissa and Abby. Beth was the one driving him crazy. He didn't know why, couldn't explain why his body tightened every time she came near.

He'd been eyeing some fresh hay tonight, thinking making love to her in the barn would be worth a little scratchiness. And that's why he needed Floyd bunking in with him.

Because the woman made him crazy.

He shifted on the bed, hoping to find some sleep soon. It wouldn't be long before the sun came up and he'd need all his control if he was going to get close to his new student.

Beth studied Jed's face the next morning at breakfast. He looked a little tired. She sniffed and raised her chin in the air. Too bad.

He'd asked for her taunting last night with his attitude. Of course, he probably didn't care two beans about her social life. But she could pretend.

Which is what she had to do. Aunt Beulah hadn't encouraged them to date much. She said men weren't to be trusted. And Beth's only real experience had proved her aunt to be right. She didn't understand men and their attitudes toward women. And she wasn't anxious to suffer the pain it would cause to demonstrate her lack of knowledge again.

Aunt Beulah said to learn a lesson the first time saved a woman a lot of tears.

Besides, it had taken most of their energy to keep the ranch going. They only had time to go to a local barn dance every once in a while. Now that they could afford not to work so hard, maybe they'd all three become social butterflies. She smiled at the thought, studying her sisters, since it seemed so unlikely.

Then her gaze ran right smack into Jed's blue eyes.

"Something amusing?" he asked.

"Nope. Just enjoying my day," she assured him, and turned her attention to her breakfast.

Jed turned to Abby. "I've got four horses arriving today. We need to work out an amount for board. And I'll work with Miss Beth two hours this morning and two this afternoon, if that's okay with you."

"Okay," Abby agreed. "I'll figure out a fair amount." Then she turned to Beth. "Can you check the herd we moved yesterday, after you finish with Jed?"

"Sure. Need me to take out some salt blocks?"

"Yeah, I think four should do it."

Jed frowned. "I can go with her. Those are heavy."

Beth saw his offer as a criticism of her, but Abby laughed. "You've got those horses coming. Don't worry. It won't be the first salt block Beth has delivered." Then she assigned various chores to her three cowboys.

It was six-thirty when everyone finished. Since she had half an hour before she was to start her training, Beth began loading the dishwasher.

"I can do that," Melissa protested.

"I've got a little spare time," she assured her sister.

Jed, the last to leave the kitchen, carried his cup to the sink. "I'll meet you in the barn."

"Right. Seven o'clock sharp," she snapped back.

"If you need more time to help Miss Melissa, take it. I'll have plenty to do while I'm waiting for you."

It was Melissa who answered him. Beth was too shocked.

"That's so sweet of you, Jed, but I can manage."

With a nod and a tip of his hat to her sister, Jed strolled out of the kitchen.

"Isn't he the sweetest person?" Melissa asked, smiling.

Beth stared at her sister. "You—you like him?"

"Of course I like him. Don't you?" Melissa asked, turning to stare at her.

"No, I mean—*like* him," Beth asked, wondering where her communication skills had disappeared to.

Melissa chuckled. "Do you mean am I turned on by his tight jeans and handsome face?"

Beth nodded, holding her breath while she waited for her sister's answer.

"I suppose I could be if I worked at it. He's handsome enough. But not really. Are you?"

Beth ducked her head, concentrating on the dishes, and lied to her sister for the first time in ages. "No, of course not."

Jed prepared for the new arrivals. Then he caught Shorty and saddled him in preparation for Beth's arrival. He was placing the barrels in the nearest pasture when he saw her approach Shorty, waiting in the nearby corral.

He automatically checked his watch, not surprised to discover it was seven o'clock on the dot. At least she was on time. He headed for the corral.

"I've set up the barrels over here. Why don't you bring Shorty over."

"Okay." She unlooped the reins and, after patting the horse on his nose, she led him after Jed.

"Walk him through the course," he ordered. He was supposed to watch the horse, but he discovered his gaze focused on Beth. She looked better in jeans than any woman he'd ever met.

When he had her swing into the saddle, Shorty lifted his head, ready to take off. "Don't run him. Just take him around the barrels easy-like."

She had started on the course as he heard a truck coming down the lane. Reluctantly he took his gaze off her delectable figure and noted the truck pulled a horse trailer. Good thing he was ready.

"I've got a customer. I'll be right back. Keep taking him through the routine."

Beth did as Jed had ordered. For the first hour. After repeating the boring pattern for that long, she thought she'd earned a little entertainment.

Just as she put her heels into Shorty's side and leaned low over the saddle, Jed stepped out of the barn. She reined in immediately, but she wasn't properly contrite.

"What are you doing?"

"Trying to relieve a little boredom," she said crisply.

"I told you to take it easy."

"I did for the past hour. But I decided that was long enough." She glared at him. As much as she was paying for his services, she thought she ought to get a little more attention.

"Was it that long?" he asked, checking his watch. "Sorry, I hadn't realized you'd been working on that pattern for so long. Go ahead, take him through it faster, but don't push him."

With a nod, she again urged Shorty forward. The picked-up pace felt good and she leaned into the turns, guiding Shorty with both her body and the reins.

When she rode back to where Jed waited, he smiled. "Did that feel better?"

"Yes," she said brusquely. She still hadn't forgiven him for abandoning her for an entire hour.

"Want to try it again, a little faster?"

With a nod, she started again.

By the time the second hour had ended, she was ready to call it quits. "Is that it?" she asked, when he signaled for her to dismount.

"Yeah. We don't want to overdo it. You going to take out the salt blocks now?"

She nodded, already leading Shorty toward the corral.

"I'll load the salt blocks into whatever truck you're driving."

She came to an abrupt halt. "I don't need any help."

He cocked one eyebrow, a trait she was already familiar with. "They're heavy."

"This is not my first experience with a salt block." She tied Shorty's reins to the corral and began unsaddling him.

"I was trying to be helpful."

Okay, so she knew that, and she should appreciate his offer, but it smacked of criticism of her ability to do a job. And that she wouldn't stand for.

"I suppose if I offered to rub Shorty down, I'd be stepping out of line again?"

She whirled around and almost fell against him. He'd sneaked up on her. "I can do my job, Jed. Don't sell me short."

"I know you can do your job, but there's no reason for you to do *all* the jobs." He smiled. "I've never seen women work as hard as you and your sisters. That doesn't mean you *should* work that hard. It'll make you old before your time."

"So now you're saying I look bad?"

He sighed, then caught her chin between his thumb and his forefinger. "Lady, what is your problem today? I've stepped in so many land mines, I'm walking on stubs. I reckon you've been told you're a beautiful woman, so that question was out-and-out ridiculous. Give me Shorty and go load your salt blocks. I've got better things to do than argue with you."

He reached over her head and untied Shorty's reins, then led the horse into the barn.

Beth drew a deep breath. The man drove her crazy. She knew she'd been difficult. She just didn't know why.

With a sigh, she pulled the keys to one of the trucks out of her pocket. Salt blocks were waiting.

Jed had received all four horses he intended to train, and he'd also fielded a couple more calls on his cellular phone. Those prospective customers wouldn't be arriving until tomorrow. He still had to visit the Stallings place and evaluate that horse.

Stallings had admitted the horse had been mistreated by a previous owner and wouldn't be an easy customer. Jed hoped he could accept the horse. He hated to consider an animal beyond hope.

With those thoughts on his mind, he was surprised by Beth's return. He frowned. She was taking the truck over the uneven ground too quickly. He stepped forward as she pulled to a stop.

"Hi," she said, the driver's window down as he drew closer.

"Something the matter?"

She seemed taken aback by his question. "No. Is everything all right here?"

"Everything's fine, as far as I know. I just figured there was a fire someplace, as fast as you were driving." He held her gaze, intent on warning her about her behavior.

The confusion on her face turned to laughter, surprising him. "You're telling me I was driving too fast?"

"Yes, I am. You could hurt yourself."

She killed the motor and slid out of the truck. "Jed Davis, I've been driving over these hills since I was twelve. In that truck. Neither of us has suffered from it." Without waiting for him to respond, she headed for the house. Halfway there, she stopped and turned to look at him. "Aren't you coming to lunch?"

"Yeah," he said, then cleared his throat. Somehow it had filled with something he couldn't define as he'd watched her swinging gait walking away from him.

Lunch. He'd better concentrate on food. Or horses. Or the weather. Anything but her.

He, Beth and Melissa had lunch at the house. Melissa had packed food for the others since they were working too far away to return for lunch. He kept his gaze on the food, only speaking when Melissa asked him questions.

Beth didn't bother talking to him at all.

When lunch was over, he returned to the barn. After checking his clipboard, he realized he'd have to return to the house for directions to the Stallings ranch. Hoping Beth had left, he started toward the house, then stopped when he heard a truck.

He frowned, knowing all the horses he'd agreed to take were already on the premises. Maybe whoever was coming was here for one of the Kennedys. He waited for the truck to come to a halt, figuring he could take a message to the house when he went for directions.

Beth's sudden appearance on the back porch, her gaze on the arriving truck, made that unnecessary. She stepped down and strode toward him.

"I thought you hadn't agreed to take their horse."

"Whose horse?" he asked.

"The Stallingses. That's their truck. And Sissy's pulling a trailer."

"I didn't agree."

He turned to stare at the new arrival, and Beth turned with him, squaring her shoulders.

A tall blonde in tight jeans appeared from behind the truck door. She completely ignored Beth as she strolled to a halt in front of Jed.

"You must be Jed Davis," she drawled, her red lips curved in a sexy smile.

"Yeah," he returned, his eyes narrowing. Beth

might turn him on, but she was no tease. Her innocence was part of her charm. This lady would never be accused of innocence.

The blonde shook her hair back and held out a hand. Jed noted the red nail polish. "I'm Sissy Stallings."

"Miss Stallings. Do you know Miss Kennedy?" He already knew the answer to that, but he wasn't going to stand for the woman ignoring Beth, as if she were invisible.

"Of course, darlin'. We're old...friends."

He gave a nod. "If you need me, Miss Beth, I'll be in the barn."

He'd turned his back on the new arrival and taken several steps toward the barn before Sissy pulled herself together to stop him.

"Wait! I mean, I came to see you, Jed."

When he turned, she had a pout on her red lips. "Me?"

"Well, of course. Daddy said he talked to you."

He stared at her, then turned his gaze to the trailer. "Your father talked to me about a gelding he wanted trained. I agreed to go see him."

"Knowing how busy you are, Daddy and I thought you'd appreciate it if we brought Mugsy to you." She beamed at him, obviously expecting his approval.

He frowned at her. "No. It would've been easier to evaluate him in his own place. If he's anything like your father described, he's going to be agitated by the ride."

Sissy looked put out. Placing her hands on her hips, she glared at him. "You want me to take him back home? We were just trying to do you a favor."

He doubted that. Instead of answering her, he turned to Beth. "Will it be all right with Miss Abby if I put him in that back corral? It'll take a couple of days for me to make my evaluation."

"I'm sure it will be all right," Beth said, looking at him.

He smiled at her generosity. She didn't like the blonde, he could tell, but she wouldn't take revenge. "Thanks," he said quietly.

"So are you going to look at him or not?" Sissy asked, stepping closer.

"Yeah, I'll look at him. Bring him out."

Her eyes widening in surprise, Sissy protested, "*I* can't unload him. He's too dangerous."

Beth shifted beside him, but she said nothing. He stared at the other woman. "You mean you brought the horse by yourself, but you're not prepared to handle him?"

"Of course not! I ride, but I don't take care of the horses. Daddy has employees to do all that stuff."

"Daddy's employees aren't here," he pointed out.

Beth chuckled. When both he and Sissy looked at her, she tried to turn it into a cough.

He frowned at Beth, but Sissy drew his attention again.

"You can unload him."

"Thanks for the opportunity," he drawled.

She shrugged. "If you don't want to bother, I'm supposed to drive him straight to the glue factory."

"I'll help," Beth immediately offered.

Jed took her arm before she could head for the trailer. "You'll do no such thing." He looked at Sissy. "Go open the gate on the corral."

She looked affronted that he'd give her an order, but he stared her down. When she finally walked away, he released his grip on Beth.

"Stay away from the trailer. This isn't going to be easy. I don't want you getting hurt."

"You let me unload Shorty," she pointed out, her chin going up.

"I knew Shorty. This horse has problems. I can unload him, but not if I'm going to have to worry about you. Stay back."

Jed gave himself plenty of time to ease the horse's fears. Even so, it took all his muscle to control the horse. Once he got him out of the trailer, he headed for the back corral.

Beth had waited to be sure he hadn't needed her help, he suspected, and now she walked with him.

"He's a pretty animal."

"He's got wild eyes."

"But—can you train him?"

"Do you want me to?" His question was low, not meant to be heard by their visitor, waiting impatiently by the corral gate.

"Not for her. But the horse doesn't deserve to be written off." She turned those fascinating hazel eyes on him, and he read the earnestness in her gaze.

Sissy Stallings used horses. Beth Kennedy loved them. Jed knew which woman mattered to him.

"We'll see what we can do," he assured her with a smile.

Once he'd turned the horse loose in the corral and fetched water and feed for him, he turned to Sissy. "Tell your father I'll let him know in a couple of days whether or not I can do anything for Mugsy."

Since the horse was now on the other side of the fence, Sissy moved closer. She pretended to brush something off his shoulder, but Jed suspected it was a pretense. He wanted to step away, but, as with all dangerous animals, he knew she'd take retreat as a sign of weakness.

"I'll tell him. And I'll come over every day to see how much progress he's making." She smiled at him.

"I'd rather you didn't. I don't like to be watched."

"Well, when I get here, you could stop work and we could...visit."

"Too busy."

"But—"

"I'll let him know." He stepped around her and headed for the barn. He didn't get far. Red talons grabbed his arm.

"Wait! I wanted to invite you to the dance."

He caught a glimpse of Beth's expression over Sissy's shoulder. Those words hadn't made her happy.

"What dance?"

"The town of Tumbleweed is having an Autumn

Affair on Friday.'' She smirked at the title of the event. ''In other words, a barn dance. We can go together, so you can meet the neighbors.''

''That's a good idea,'' he said slowly, his gaze on Beth, ''but I can't accept your invitation.''

It was clear Miss Sissy Stallings didn't often get rejected. She stamped her foot. ''Why not?''

''I've already got a date.''

Chapter Six

Beth tried to hide the pleasure Jed's answer gave her. Especially when Sissy whirled around to stare at her.

"I should've known you'd get your claws into him as soon as you could," she spat toward Beth.

Beth grinned and shrugged her shoulders. She knew Jed didn't mean her, but she wasn't going to inform Sissy of that fact.

Sissy turned back to Jed. "When you get tired of Miss Hayseed, here, let me know. I'll show you how a real woman entertains her man." With those words, she flounced back to the truck.

Neither Beth nor Jed moved until the truck and trailer had left a plume of dust in its wake. Then, as if released from a spell, they looked at each other.

Beth giggled. "You sure showed her."

"What did I show her?"

Beth's smile grew even wider. "That you didn't fall for her—her—" She broke off, unsure what to call Sissy's brand of flirtation.

"Uh-huh. Do you realize we have a problem?"

Beth stared at him, unable to read the expression in his blue eyes. "We do?"

He nodded. "She thinks I'm taking you to the dance."

Beth's amusement immediately fled. Nibbling on her bottom lip, she thought about Jed's words. It wasn't that she hadn't realized what Sissy thought. She had. But she hadn't thought ahead. She hadn't thought about what Sissy would say when Jed arrived with someone else.

"Who are you taking?" she finally asked.

"I had Floyd in mind. I thought we'd check things out together. If he wants to." Jed put his hands on his hips and stared at her. "That woman is going to act ugly no matter what, I guess, but I sure hate for her to rip you to shreds with your neighbors."

Her breathing sped up as she stared at the sexy man opposite her. "You—you could be a gentleman and save me."

"How could I do that?" he asked, his eyes narrowing.

He was stalling and she knew it. Taking a step closer to him, she said, "You could take *me*."

He frowned ferociously, as if her words were a surprise. "I don't like to mix business and pleasure."

She wanted to ask him which he considered her to be, but she didn't. She wouldn't like the answer.

"Since we'd both know you were only doing it to protect me, I don't think it would hurt." No need to mention she'd faced these situations with Sissy Stallings for years and lived to tell about them.

He rubbed the back of his neck, then looked at her again. "I suppose I could, as long as you understand there's nothing personal. And—and you'd better explain to Miss Abby and Miss Melissa. I don't want them getting the wrong idea."

She rolled her eyes. "You could just wear a string of garlic around your neck. I think that would tell everyone what you think of me."

He grinned. "I could...but none of the other ladies would dance with me."

She wanted to choke his neck. Instead, she sauntered closer. "If you don't dance better than you flirt, they probably won't anyway." Then she stepped around him and hurried to the house.

It was so satisfying to have the last word.

Jed worked hard all afternoon. First he found Abby and asked to cut out six young steers to take to one of the corrals. The four horses he'd taken in, other than Mugsy, were to be trained as cutting horses. He couldn't do that without a small herd.

By the time he drove them back to the corral and penned them up, it was time for Beth's second lesson. Not that he was anxious to see her. Of course not. He'd watched the time only to see if she'd be late.

The sigh of relief—and maybe anticipation—that

ran through his body when he saw her step off the back porch was only concern about his work. Since she wore a sunny smile, he thought letting her have the last word earlier had been a smart move on his part.

They got through the two hours without any disagreements. Of course, they hardly talked. She went through the course over and over again. He saw the frustration build in her, but he believed the discipline of training paid off in the end.

"All right, this is your last run-through," he told her, pulling a stopwatch out of his pocket. "Let 'er rip."

"You mean it?" she demanded, her face lighting up.

"Yeah, but be careful."

Before the words were out of his mouth, she'd jammed her hat hard on her head and bent low over the saddle. Then she signaled Shorty to go like the wind.

Jed watched her, his heart in his throat. The lady did nothing at half-speed, if given a choice. He hoped he hadn't cut her loose too soon. When she raced across the finish line he'd marked, he clicked the stopwatch.

Her time was better already than most riders. But he'd picked up on several things he thought would improve it. Yeah, he'd picked a winner with Beth Kennedy. She was going to do him proud.

"How'd I do?" she asked eagerly.

"Not bad. We've got some things to work on, but not bad."

Her grin disappeared. "Well, don't fall all over yourself complimenting me."

"I might, if you could ride as well as you flirt," he assured her with a grin. Then he walked away.

It was his turn for the last word.

Two nights later, the Kennedy household was as busy as a beehive as three ladies all got ready at the same time for the local Autumn Affair.

"Is Jed picking you up?" Abby called from the bath where she was curling her hair with a curling iron.

"He said he'd come by about seven," Beth returned. She'd dutifully told Abby and Melissa about Sissy's spitefulness, not a surprise to either of them. Then she'd explained about Jed's gentlemanly offer.

"Do you think that's wise?" Abby had asked. "After all, he is your instructor."

Having fought the butterflies in her stomach all day, Beth didn't bother to justify what was happening. "Probably not, but when presented with an opportunity to spite Sissy, I'm not going to turn it down."

Melissa grinned. "Yeah, and it'll be such a chore to dance with poor old ugly Jed."

Beth's cheeks flamed. "Yeah, but I'll make the sacrifice." They had all laughed.

She'd also sacrificed yesterday afternoon to drive into Wichita Falls to the mall and find new clothes to wear. She'd even gotten her hair trimmed and had a manicure. Her nails weren't long, like Sissy's, and she didn't choose red polish. But they looked nice with a soft shell-pink color on them.

To match her polish, she'd found a scoop-necked blouse, a silver concho belt and a short denim skirt. She'd been told she had nice legs. She wanted to look her best so Jed Davis would know what he was missing when he stuck to business.

She came out of her bedroom, ready to go, and faced her sisters. "Well?"

"Oh, my," Melissa said, staring at her.

"Isn't that skirt a little short?" Abby demanded.

"It's only a couple of inches above my knees," Beth justified.

"It just looks shorter because we're all tall," Melissa said. "And she does look good. Those cowboys are going to be following her around all night."

Abby sighed. "I feel like an old hen letting her only chick out for the first time."

Beth laughed. "Well, you don't look all that old, and just because your skirt is longer doesn't mean you don't look sexy, too. Both of you are going to attract a lot of attention."

A rap on the back door drew Beth's attention and wiped the smile from her face. "I—I guess that's Jed."

Her sisters nodded and moved aside, letting her go down the stairs in front of them.

Licking her lips, Beth hurried to the back door and swung it open. Jed had on pressed jeans, a royal blue shirt that made his eyes all the more sexy, and he wore an almost new Stetson on his head.

He was as handsome as sin.

Damn if she wasn't all legs.

By the time his gaze reached the top of her blouse, way south of her chin, he knew he was in big trouble. He'd thought she was dang near perfect in jeans. She took on angel status in a skirt.

A sexy angel.

"Uh, you ready to go?"

"Yes," she said in a whisper. "I'll just get my sweater." October in the panhandle of Texas could be brisk.

She seemed surprised when he took the sweater from her and held it out for her to slip her arms into. It was a blue knit.

"You'd think we coordinated our clothes," he said with a frown.

"You're not wearing pink," she pointed out.

His grin relieved a little of the tension. "Well, no. Men don't wear pink. But your sweater's blue, like my shirt and we're both wearing denim."

"So will everyone else. The denim, I mean."

He nodded and backed toward the door. He held it open for her, standing as far away as he could. Getting close to Beth in that outfit would be dangerous. He'd considered asking Floyd to accompany the two of them, but the memory of her pressed against him all the way back from Oklahoma had discouraged that idea.

Thank God.

He opened the passenger door to his newly washed truck.

"You cleaned the truck!" she exclaimed.

"You act surprised."

"Well, I mean, I didn't know if you'd have time."

"I had time." Cinderella couldn't go to the ball in a dirty coach. He might not be Prince Charming, but he was going to do his best not to let her down.

Beth drew a deep breath just before Jed opened the door to the barn dance. The tension had built during their ride, neither of them speaking. Now she had to face her neighbors…and Sissy Stallings.

When Jed's arm snaked around her waist, she expelled the pent-up air and stared at him. "What are you doing?"

"Escorting you into the hall, darlin'," he assured her with a rakish cowboy grin. She'd seen that kind of grin before, but never on Jed Davis's face.

Good thing, too.

It was high-voltage and made her want to curl up against his hard body. In privacy.

Hellos rang out as she unconsciously moved into the hall, her gaze still on Jed. Her head snapped around and she fought the blush that filled her cheeks, greeting everyone.

A number of them stepped forward to be introduced to Jed. It was clear they all knew who he was. His reputation had preceded him. Of course, that didn't explain why all the women under the age of thirty, and a few who were questionable, managed to drop by to greet Beth and wait for her to perform the introductions.

The dancing had already started before the crowd had dispersed. In fact, one determined young lady asked Jed to join her on the dance floor.

Beth couldn't believe Susie McCaskin's gall.

Except that she was seventeen and thought she was the hottest woman in the county. She was...at the high school. Beth held her breath again for Jed's response.

"I appreciate the offer, Susie, but I think it would be rude not to have the first dance with my date." He'd kept his arm around her waist and now he squeezed it.

Beth wasn't sure what he was trying to communicate, but she supposed he wanted support. "I would be a little irritated, Susie. Maybe later—"

"I imagine Miss Susie's dance card will be all filled by then, darlin'," Jed said with a smile aimed at the young lady.

She wasn't appeased. With red cheeks, she turned and began flirting with the nearest cowboy.

"I think you hurt her feelings," Beth whispered.

"Good. She needs to grow up a little before she starts playing with the big boys." He swung her into his arms and moved onto the dance floor for some Texas two-step.

Many female gazes followed them, but Beth stopped letting the attention bother her when she realized what a good dancer Jed was.

"You're a great dancer!" she whispered, staring at his tanned, square-jawed face. She'd figured he seldom went dancing. He'd always appeared all business.

"Thanks," he drawled, obviously having heard the compliment before. "One of my foster mothers liked to dance."

She almost fell over her feet. She hadn't realized she and Jed had something in common. "You were orphaned?"

He raised his eyebrows, as if questioning why her feet hadn't followed his. "Yeah. You all right?"

"I—I didn't know—we were orphaned, too."

He gave a cynical laugh. "Yeah, and fell right into the berry patch. That's a hard life, lady."

"What do you mean?"

"Hell, Beth, I mean, Miss Beth, you're a millionaire. Don't expect a lot of sympathy."

Gone was the building attraction, the fascination with his...his maleness. Instead, she experienced the loss, the confusion, the sadness of a nine-year-old child when her happy world suddenly ended.

She broke from his arms and strode across the dance floor, looking for her sisters.

"Dear, are you all right?"

She came to a halt, faced with Mrs. Wisner, one of their neighbors. She and her husband had lived on a small farm across the road from their ranch. Mr. Wisner had died a year ago.

"Hello, Mrs. Wisner. I'm fine. But I was looking for Melissa and Abby." She tried a wobbly smile.

The lady offered a sympathetic smile. "They're dancing, like you were."

Jed stepped to her side, and Beth flinched as he slid his arm around her waist. "Hello. I'm Jed Davis," he said, offering his other hand to Mrs. Wisner.

"I'm Ellen Wisner, a neighbor. Welcome to our little community."

"Thanks. Beth, you want something to drink?"

She wouldn't look at him. With her body stiff, she shook her head no.

Hell, he hadn't intended to hurt her feelings. But there was no pussyfooting around it. His being orphaned was a different thing from hers.

"Come on, Beth, don't—"

Ellen Wisner interrupted his impatient words. "Why don't you bring both of us a glass of punch, Mr. Davis. I'd really appreciate it."

Her gentle smile was impossible to refuse.

She reminded him of the kind of mother he'd always wanted. Someone who could make everything better. However, she wasn't his mother, probably wasn't even old enough. But maybe she'd help Beth get over her snit.

He nodded and walked to the big table set up at one end. Several ladies, considerably older than Ellen Wisner, waited to serve him. "Three glasses of punch, please. Is there a charge?"

One of the ladies giggled. "Oh, no, dearie. It's all part of the price of admission."

As they set out three cups of punch, he realized

he'd have difficulty managing all three cups. He looked around and saw Floyd standing to one side with Barney. He waved him over before turning to the ladies. "I need one more cup, please."

"How's it goin', boy?" Floyd asked with a grin when he reached the table.

Instead of answering him, Jed handed him two cups of punch. "Follow me."

When he reached Beth and Mrs. Wisner, they were sitting in chairs against the wall, talking quietly. He handed each of them a cup. Then he turned to Floyd and took one of the cups from him. "Thanks, Floyd. Let me introduce you to Ellen Wisner."

Floyd shook hands with the lady. Then he sat down in the chair next to Ellen. "You don't mind me sitting here, I hope."

"Why, no, if Beth doesn't mind."

Jed sat down next to Beth and she stared straight ahead, not acknowledging his presence. "Beth," he whispered, leaning closer.

She shifted away from him. The music stopped. Amid the general clapping, Beth sprang to her feet. "I need to find my sisters."

Then she bolted across the room, leaving Jed sitting there. "Damn."

"What'd you do?" Floyd asked.

"He hurt her feelings," Ellen said softly, when Jed didn't answer.

When he glared at her, she added, "Men can be so insensitive." Her smile widened.

Floyd chuckled. "It's 'cause we don't understand you women, honey."

"Oh!" Ellen exclaimed, "That's what my husband used to call me." Her eyes filled with tears and she jumped up, following Beth's escape route.

"Hey, we're really slick, pal," Floyd said, disgust on his face. "The two prettiest ladies in the room, and we send them both running."

"Yeah." Things were going downhill fast.

Abby and Melissa had surrounded Beth, anxious to be sure she was all right. Their partners offered to beat up Jed if it was necessary, even though they didn't know what was wrong.

Beth hurriedly shook her head, feeling foolish. "Oh, no, I'm being silly. There's nothing—" Her gaze landed on Ellen hurrying away, looking terribly sad. Beth's brows lowered. Jed might hurt her feelings. She'd recover. But he sure wasn't going to hurt sweet Mrs. Wisner.

"Excuse me," she muttered, and hurried after the lady.

"Mrs. Wisner?" she called, catching Ellen's arm. "Are you okay? Did Jed say something mean?"

Ellen blinked rapidly. "Oh, no. That nice Mr. Jenkins—he called me honey." Her cheeks were rosy and she looked ten years younger.

Beth didn't know how to respond. Was that good or bad? So she took Ellen's hand in hers and waited.

"My—my husband used to call me that. I—I've

been so lonely.'' Ellen shook her head and looked away. "I'm a foolish old woman.''

"You're definitely not old,'' Beth said, suddenly realizing what she said was true. Aunt Beulah had talked about baby-sitting Ellen Wisner when she was a baby. "Why don't you ask him to dance?''

Once the idea struck Beth, she didn't wait for an answer. Taking Ellen's hand, she hauled her back across the floor. The two men hadn't moved, but their heads were hanging down, and they didn't see them approach.

"Floyd, would you do me a favor?'' Beth asked.

Both men's heads snapped up. Then they jumped to their feet. Floyd responded at once. "Sure.''

"Beth, I didn't mean to—'' Jed began until she turned and glared at him.

After he was silenced, she looked at Floyd, not turning loose of Ellen. "Would you ask Ellen to dance?''

"Beth, you mustn't—please don't—'' Ellen protested.

"Ma'am, I'd be delighted to dance with you if you promise not to complain about my dancin'. I'm no Fred Astaire,'' Floyd said, smiling eagerly.

Even Ellen couldn't think he didn't want to dance with her, with that look on his face. Beth beamed at the two of them as they moved out onto the dance floor.

Leaving her and Jed alone.

Chapter Seven

"So," he asked, "are you going to forgive me?"

Jed didn't realize how important her answer was until she shrugged her shoulders and replied, "There's nothing to forgive."

But since she still wouldn't look at him, he wasn't fooled into believing her. About to plead his case again, he was interrupted by a cowboy halting in front of them.

"Hey, Beth, how about a dance?"

Jed squared his shoulders, wanting to protest but knowing better. Beth had the right to dance with anyone she wished. She accepted the invitation with a smile.

He slumped into his chair, his gaze fixed on Beth's long bare legs, her small waist emphasized by the silver belt, her dark hair curling on her shoulders. Her pink nails.

Here's a **HOT** offer for you!

Get set for a sizzling summer read...

with **2 FREE ROMANCE BOOKS**
and a **FREE MYSTERY GIFT!**
NO CATCH! NO OBLIGATION TO BUY!

Simply complete and return this card and you'll get **2 FREE BOOKS** and **A FREE GIFT** – yours to keep!

Visit us online at www.eHarlequin.com

- The first shipment is yours to keep, **absolutely free!**

- Enjoy the convenience of Silhouette Romance® books delivered right to your door, before they're available in stores!

- Take advantage of special low pricing for **Reader Service Members only!**

- After receiving your free books we hope you'll want to remain a subscriber. But the choice is always yours—to continue or cancel, any time at all! So why not take us up on this fabulous invitation, with no risk of any kind. You'll be glad you did!

315 SDL C26P

215 SDL C26K
(S-R-OS-06/00)

▼ DETACH HERE AND MAIL CARD TODAY! ▼

Name: _____
(Please Print)

Address: _____ Apt.#: _____

City: _____

State/Prov.: _____ Zip/Postal Code: _____

The Silhouette Reader Service™ —Here's how it works:

Accepting your 2 free books and gift places you under no obligation to buy anything. You may keep the books and gift and return the shipping statement marked "cancel." If you do not cancel, about a month later we'll send you 6 additional novels and bill you just $2.90 each in the U.S., or $3.25 each in Canada, plus 25¢ delivery per book and applicable taxes if any.* That's the complete price and — compared to cover prices of $3.50 each in the U.S. and $3.99 each in Canada — it's quite a bargain! You may cancel at any time, but if you choose to continue, every month we'll send you 6 more books, which you may either purchase at the discount price or return to us and cancel your subscription.

*Terms and prices subject to change without notice. Sales tax applicable in N.Y. Canadian residents will be charged applicable provincial taxes and GST.

If offer card is missing write to: Silhouette Reader Service, 3010 Walden Ave., P.O. Box 1867, Buffalo, NY 14240-1867

BUSINESS REPLY MAIL
FIRST-CLASS MAIL   PERMIT NO. 717   BUFFALO, NY

POSTAGE WILL BE PAID BY ADDRESSEE

SILHOUETTE READER SERVICE
3010 WALDEN AVE
PO BOX 1867
BUFFALO NY 14240-9952

NO POSTAGE
NECESSARY
IF MAILED
IN THE
UNITED STATES

Her pink nails? Damn, she'd gotten a manicure.

"Regretting your decision?" Sissy Stallings asked, sliding into the chair next to him.

He hadn't seen her since they'd arrived, and he'd forgotten about the supposed reason for his bringing Beth to the dance. "Nope."

"Why isn't she dancing with you?"

"Because the guy asked her to dance. Why aren't you dancing?" As far as he could tell, the men outnumbered the ladies at least two to one. And Sissy, even if she was bitchy, was a beauty.

"I was looking for you. Come on, join me." She stood and held out her hand.

He didn't want to. He knew he shouldn't. But Beth hadn't hesitated to sashay onto the floor with another cowboy. He stood and led Sissy to the dance floor.

The fast music made it easy to maneuver Sissy across the floor next to Beth and her partner. He kept his eye on Beth and knew the moment she caught sight of him and Sissy. She stiffened, then raised her chin and stared at him.

"What are you looking at?" Sissy asked, twisting her head in the same direction. "Oh, hi, Beth, Billy."

Jed wasn't going to back off now. He turned loose of Sissy and tapped Billy on the shoulder. "Trade partners." Then he pulled Beth out of her partner's arms and wrapped his around her. He didn't look back to see if Billy took Sissy as his partner. She was a big girl. She could take care of herself.

"What do you think you're doing?"

He smiled down at the delicate rigid features. "I'm

claiming my partner, sweetheart. You're the one who suggested we come together. The least you can do is dance with me.''

"If I dance only with you, we'll be engaged before the night is over," she snapped.

"Well, I don't want to go that far, but a little friendliness wouldn't be amiss." He didn't think his sin was so serious she should avoid him. And she felt good in his arms.

Pulling her more tightly against him, he laid his cheek on the top of her head, taking in the delicate scent of her hair.

"Jed."

"Mmm-hmm?" he answered, savoring the feel of her.

"You're holding me too close," she complained, but her voice was breathless rather than irritated.

"This kind of dance requires it." Or maybe his heart required it. No. Not his heart. His body. Man, he wanted her bad.

Suddenly he stepped back and pulled her after him, off the dance floor. He needed some air. Unfortunately, his body needed some distance from hers or he was going to embarrass himself.

"We must be destined not to finish a dance," she said, tugging on his hand.

He muttered, "Sorry. I got hot."

She raised her eyebrows.

"I mean, the room is hot. It's hot in here. I need some air.''

With a giggle, she suddenly relaxed for the first

time since they had arrived. "Okay, let's get some air."

He followed her to the front door, wondering if he'd ever understand the woman. She'd been distraught over his dismissal of her anguish, something he regretted. But she'd been amused that she made him hot.

Fortunately, there was no darkness outside, no temptation to take her back into his arms and kiss the daylights out of her. Instead, there were spotlights everywhere, and forty or fifty men were standing around chatting.

"Mr. Dawkins, let me introduce Jed Davis," Beth said to a neighbor. In no time, the men had surrounded Jed, asking him questions about his rodeo career and his training techniques.

He slid an arm around Beth, preventing her from abandoning him, and answered their questions. He'd rather be holding her, but talking to these men was a lot safer.

Beth could not believe how the evening had gone so far. She had yet to finish a dance. And she was outside chatting with the older men, talking about crop rotation, horse training and the weather.

And after she'd gone to so much trouble with her appearance.

Of course, she *had* turned Jed Davis on.

That would be a feather in her cap, if she hadn't also set her own motor racing. The man was lethal to a woman's control.

And she still had to face the drive home.

Just when she'd decided to slip away and catch a ride home with her sisters, Jed took her hand.

"Gentlemen, I've enjoyed talking to you, but I think I owe Beth another dance, so if you'll excuse us...?" With nods of approval from his audience, he led her back toward the door.

"Sorry, if you were bored to tears," he whispered.

She hadn't been. In fact, it had been interesting seeing the respect with which the older men greeted Jed's remarks. She knew he was good. He was certainly in demand. But he had also earned a lot of respect.

"No, I'm fine. In fact, I can ride home with my sisters if you want to—"

"Do you want to go home already? Can't we at least finish one dance first?"

"Of course. I just thought you might want to—I mean, some of those people might have horses for you to train."

"I already have six horses, plus Mugsy. That's enough."

"What are you going to do about Mugsy?" She'd watched Jed stop by the corral and talk to the horse, even offer him some carrots, but she hadn't seen him go inside.

He sighed. But before he answered, they'd reached the dance floor again and he wrapped his arms around her.

It amazed her how much she liked being in his arms. She laid her head on his shoulder.

"I don't know what to do. The horse is going to be a long-term project, and I doubt Stallings will want to pay a lot."

She lifted her head. "You mean the horse will be destroyed?" She couldn't hide the anguish that thought caused her.

He pulled her tight against him. "I don't know, sweetheart."

They got to finish the dance, lost in their own little world. At least Beth was. She never wanted to leave his arms. When he finally led her from the dance floor, she was disappointed when the fiddler, piano and guitar players took a break.

"Hey, Jed Davis. I'm Dave Stallings," a big man said, approaching them with his hand extended. Beth knew the man, of course, but she hadn't had much to do with him.

"Mr. Stallings."

"What have you got to say about that gelding? Good of Sissy to bring him over, wasn't it?" He beamed at Jed, and Beth sighed. She couldn't get away from the Stallingses tonight.

"How about I call you tomorrow, Mr. Stallings, and we'll talk about Mugsy," Jed said, his voice calm, but Beth felt him tense.

"We can talk here. I figure you've had enough time to decide. Can you fix him?"

Jed muttered an apology to Beth, then turned back to Stallings. "I can, eventually, but it will take six or eight months. Even if I'm around that long, I'm not sure you'll want to pay for that much care."

"Damn right I won't. That horse isn't worth more'n two or three hundred dollars," the man snapped.

"He's not worth that much if he can't be ridden."

"Fine! I'll turn him into glue."

Beth gasped and reached out to her neighbor. "No, Mr. Stallings, please don't."

"None of that soft stuff, girl. I don't let my Sissy get sentimental about animals. I'm not going to let another filly mess in my business."

"I'll buy him," she said, suddenly finding an answer.

The speculative glint in the man's eyes told Beth he was calculating his profits. "Well, now, a fine horse like that, I reckon I couldn't let him go for less than eight hundred dollars."

Beth was nodding in agreement, when Jed stepped in. "You said the horse wasn't worth more than two or three hundred, and only then if he's broken in."

"Well, the market just improved."

"No, it didn't. You'll get fifty dollars for him at the glue factory. Pick him up tomorrow."

"Jed!" Beth protested.

"Hey, you can't interfere," Stallings protested.

Jed startled Beth by leaning down and wrapping his arms around her for a hug before he looked at the other man. "Oh, yeah, I can. If you want to sell the horse to Beth, she'll pay you two hundred, which will be more than he's worth. Otherwise, there's no deal. By the way, you'll need at least two cowboys to get him loaded in a trailer."

He swung Beth around, as if she had no will at all, and started off in the opposite direction.

"Wait!" Stallings called.

Beth had been on the verge of elbowing Jed and whispering frantic protests in his ear. But she decided to wait for whatever Sissy's father wanted.

"Okay, you've got a deal. But I want my money tomorrow," the man growled.

Beth couldn't believe her ears. She would have hugged Jed, if he hadn't been holding her so tightly she couldn't move. But she could talk. "You'll have a check tomorrow."

Jed reached into his back pocket. He pulled out a checkbook. "You'll have your check tonight."

"Jed, I can pay—"

"We'll settle up later," he said firmly, as if to ensure she agreed.

"Now, wait a minute. Who's buying the horse? Are you trying to trick me? Did you lie to me about how bad off he is?"

Jed stiffened, his shoulders rigid. Pressed against him, Beth could feel his reaction. "Stallings, no one calls my integrity into question. Do what you want with your horse."

"Okay, okay. Give me the check." There was a crowd gathering around, and clearly the man didn't want any reaction from his neighbors.

Jed released Beth and borrowed a pen from a man standing nearby. After he'd handed a check to Stallings, he added, "We'll expect a bill of sale."

"Sure, sure. I'll send it over." He glared at Beth.

"You just wasted your money, little lady. But easy come, easy go." And he stalked off.

Beth felt as though she'd been run over by a truck. But slowly she realized she'd just bought herself a horse. She turned to Jed, beaming at him.

Before she could thank him, however, he glared at her. "You are determined to throw away your money."

All the good feelings she ever had about Jed disappeared. "What? Why are you angry?"

"I told you about throwing away your money, letting people jack up the price. Didn't you learn anything?"

Floyd, holding Ellen's hand, stepped up, laying his hand on Jed's shoulder. "Hey, pal, don't be so rough on the little lady."

Ellen reached out a hand and touched Beth's arm. "Are you all right?"

Oh, yeah, she was all right. But she wasn't happy. She smiled at Ellen, then stiffened her features and faced the bane of her existence. "If you're worried I won't pay you, I'll write you a check as soon as we get home. Plus a month's training in advance."

"Damn it, you think I'm a money-grubber like Stallings?" he asked, his voice rising in irritation.

"Then why are you angry?" she demanded.

"Because you have no sense!" he growled.

"Oh, really! Well, you have no—"

"Beth," Abby called, breaking into her retort. "What's wrong?"

"Nothing! I just bought a horse."

Abby looked confused, and Beth couldn't blame her. Her emotions had been on a roller-coaster ride ever since Jed had agreed to bring her to the dance. "I'm ready to go home."

Abby stared at her, and Jed stepped forward. Before he could speak, however, Beth added, "With you, Abby. Are you and Melissa ready?"

Abby looked at Jed, who was staring at Beth, then at her. "Sure, Beth, if you want. There's Melissa, coming over now. Melissa, are you ready to go home? Beth would like to—to leave."

Melissa and Abby exchanged a look, but both nodded in agreement. Before Beth knew what was happening, the three of them were in the pickup and heading for home.

And hopefully a return to sanity.

Jed ignored the sympathetic looks around him. He was the one in the right. The woman had no sense. She was asking to be taken. Stallings would have jacked the price up to a thousand, left to himself, and the horse might never be ridable.

"Jed, you all right?" Floyd asked.

Jed glared at his friend. "Of course, I'm all right. I was only trying to warn the woman. Her heart's too soft. She needs to toughen up."

"But that's what makes her so special," Ellen said softly, leaning toward him. "Beth cares for those around her."

"If she doesn't start caring less, she'll run out of money," he growled.

"Money isn't that important to Beth," Ellen returned, challenging him with her gaze.

"That's easy to say when you've got plenty." His voice was low but rough.

"Hey, back off, Jed," Floyd protested, putting his arm about Ellen's shoulders.

"Sorry, Mrs. Wisner, but she needs to learn—"

"Maybe she's not the only one who needs to learn something," Ellen said, again softly, before turning around and walking to the other side of the dance floor.

"Want a ride home, Floyd?" Jed asked, his gaze fixed on the older woman, wondering what she meant.

"Nope, Ellen's offered me a ride home. She's a lot sweeter than you."

Great, Jed thought as Floyd followed Ellen. I've even been abandoned by the only friend I've got around here. And he was only trying to teach Beth to—to what? Stand up for herself? She did that already. To not be fleeced by a crook? Maybe that was what he'd had in mind.

Jed turned and walked out into the night, barely responding to the chorus of goodbyes that followed him.

He'd worried about the ride home with Beth, the saying good-night on her back porch. The possible kiss.

Didn't have to worry now. No sirree. He'd taken care of all those problems. Handy, how he managed to chase those problems away.

Now all he had to worry about was how he was going to get to sleep before dawn when his body craved touching her. And he longed to hear her voice.

Yeah, this had been some night.

Even though the next day was Saturday, life went on as usual on a ranch. Jed considered skipping breakfast the next morning, but he refused to call himself a coward, so he followed the other men to the kitchen.

They were all surprised to discover Abby and Beth putting breakfast together.

''Where's Miss Melissa?'' Jed asked, frowning.

''She's not feeling well this morning,'' Abby answered. ''We told her to stay in bed. So breakfast won't be as good as usual.'' She smiled an apology.

Beth never looked at him. But she was occupied with a large skillet of eggs.

After eating, the men scattered to their assigned tasks. Beth, without looking at him, said she'd have to skip her training this morning to take care of Melissa and her chores.

''No problem. Can I help?''

That question brought her gaze to his face, but she hurriedly looked away. ''No, thank you. I can manage.''

Jed hesitated, but when she continued to ignore him, he excused himself and headed for the barn. Stubborn woman! Maybe she preferred working in the house to barrel racing.

He knew better. He'd seen the enthusiasm on Beth's face when she and Shorty raced between the barrels. She sure hadn't shown any enthusiasm this morning, faced with all the dirty dishes, preparing lunch and tending to her sister. But she did what had to be done.

That was a quality he could admire. Among other things. An immediate flash of how she had looked last night ran through his mind, but he immediately dismissed it. Beth looked good all the time. Last night had been a bonus.

A bonus. He sighed and began cleaning out stalls, feeding his animals. This job had a lot more complications than others. All because of Beth Kennedy.

He spent the morning working with the animals, but he operated on automatic pilot as his mind remained on Beth. He wanted to dismiss his anger last night as well earned. But he couldn't. Normally he never lost his temper. Training horses had taught him how damaging it could be.

Last night, when he'd seen Beth throw herself into the breach to save Mugsy, he'd overreacted. He'd wanted to protect her. But she was an adult.

He tried to dismiss his thoughts. Time to get on with his job. He saddled one of the horses and entered the corral with the young steers. After working the animal for an hour, he unsaddled it and rubbed it down, then saddled the next horse.

Then he took a break and approached Mugsy, the horse Beth had bought last night. He was afraid he'd misled Beth. It was possible the animal would never be ridable. He pulled several carrots out of his back pocket. He always kept a stash in the barn for his training.

Mugsy had taken a carrot from him for the first time yesterday. It had taken half an hour of coaxing and patience, but it had encouraged Jed.

Today, when he relaxed against the corral fence and dangled the carrot from his hands, he got the horse's attention at once. The gelding shifted, moving away from Jed, then moving closer. After several times of advancing and retreating, the horse came close enough to snatch the carrot from his hand.

Immediately Mugsy backed away, keeping an eye on Jed as he crunched the carrot.

Jed crooned to the horse, trying to get him used to his voice. After a few minutes, he returned to the training of the other horses.

And thinking about Beth.

Shortly before it was time to break for lunch, he caught a shadow of movement out of the corner of his eye. Abruptly he rode his horse closer to the end of the corral to make sure he hadn't been fooled by a shadow.

Beth in jeans. He loved her in jeans. About to call out a greeting, he noticed an air of secrecy about her. He quietly moved to the gate of the corral he was using and unlatched it, riding the horse out before he closed it again.

Then he eased his mount toward the last corral, trailing after Beth.

His breath caught in his throat as she reached the

corral where Mugsy was penned up, her hand reaching for the latch on the gate.

With taut anger, he ordered, "Don't even think about it."

Chapter Eight

Beth jumped, her grip slipping from the gate latch. "Oh! You scared me."

"I intended to. Were you planning on going in the corral?"

Staring at Jed, Beth acknowledged to herself that part of her desire to look at Mugsy was a wish to prove that she hadn't made a mistake in offering to buy the horse. That this man's anger last night wasn't justified. With her chin up, she continued to stare at him even as she nodded.

"Damn it, Beth, you know better. That horse is wild, unpredictable. You could be hurt."

She refused to let him intimidate her. "I wanted to look at my purchase."

"Look all you want...from this side of the rails."

Turning her back to him, she stared at the horse,

hovering on the far side of the corral. "You work for me, not the other way around."

From the creak of leather, she assumed he was dismounting. She kept her back to him.

Then muscular arms settled on the top rail of the corral, and his big body filled the corner of her line of vision.

"That can be remedied," he said softly.

Her head whirled around to discover him staring at the horse. "You want to quit?" she demanded.

"Nope. But if I'm to work with that horse, then you'll follow my rules. There'll be no compromises."

She considered telling him what he could do with his rules. She really did. But that would be cutting off her nose to spite her face. The man had customers lined up. It wouldn't matter to him. But she'd be stuck with a horse that couldn't be ridden.

"All right."

"All right, what?" he said, his voice still soft.

"Your rules, your way. Does that satisfy you?" She was staring at that strong profile when he shifted and faced her.

"Darlin', we don't want to discuss my satisfaction...but I'll accept the terms."

A different satisfaction filled her head and she took a step backward, her cheeks red. "I'll give you a check at lunch."

"You can give me the two hundred I paid last night, but there'll be no charge on training him until

I can get in the corral with him. You'll be taking care of the board.''

"Fine,'' she said, and backed away again. He was more dangerous than the horse in the corral. Every time she got close to him, all she could think about was his holding her. "I have to go put lunch on the table.''

"I'll be in to help as soon as I unsaddle my horse,'' he said, surprising her.

"You don't have to—''

"I won't be too long.'' Without waiting for her to respond, he grabbed the reins of the horse he'd been training and walked toward the barn.

"Well, fine,'' she sputtered. "We'll see if you're as handy at setting the table as you are at training horses.''

Of course, he didn't hear her. But the words made her feel better.

When everyone had arrived for lunch, they ate in silence, as they usually did. Hungry men and women didn't bother much with conversation. However, as they finished the lasagna Beth had warmed up, Floyd asked, "How's Miss Melissa?''

"The doctor came this morning. He's taken some blood to run tests.'' Beth looked at her sister. She'd hoped to talk to her after lunch, in private. "He thinks it might be…mononucleosis.''

"The kissing disease?'' Barney asked in surprise.

Jed cleared his throat. "Uh, there are other ways…''

"Yes,'' Abby hurriedly said, though she was fighting a smile. Until she thought about what Beth had said. She turned to her sister with a panicky look. "Mono?"

"Yeah," Beth said with a dispirited sigh.

Jed leaned forward. "Hey, don't take it so hard. She'll get some medicine and be fine."

Beth and Abby exchanged looks. Finally Beth took it upon herself to explain. "It's not concern for Melissa, Jed. I mean, we're concerned for Melissa, of course, but we know she'll get better. It's—that is, you—it's the cooking, the housekeeping, the—oh, I don't know. All the things that Melissa does. She won't be able to do them."

"But with Floyd here to help out, you can spend more time in the house."

Everyone but Floyd and Jed laughed.

"What's so funny?" Floyd asked.

"Me," Beth said. "I'm what's funny. The only reason you had a decent lunch today is Melissa had made the lasagna and frozen it. Even I can thaw something out. But there's not much in the freezer."

"You don't cook?" Jed asked.

Beth felt her cheeks heat up again. She was going to have to stop blushing around Jed. But she hated admitting such a weakness. She shook her head.

Jed frowned but didn't say anything. Everyone around the table seemed glum. She didn't blame them. One of the perks of the job was Melissa's cooking.

"I have a solution," Floyd said, surprising everyone.

Abby grinned at him. "Don't tell me you cook, Floyd."

"No, ma'am. Oh, I wouldn't starve to death, but it wouldn't be anything you'd want to eat."

Beth studied him. "Then how do you have a solution?"

"I bet Ellen Wisner is a good cook."

Abby blinked in surprise. "Well, yes, she is, but what does that have to do with anything?"

"I think she's had a tough time since her husband died. She'd probably appreciate a job."

Beth and Abby exchanged surprised looks. Beth whispered, "I never thought that she might need— are you sure, Floyd?"

"No, but I think that's the situation."

Abby abruptly stood. "I'll find out." She headed for her office, two doors down the hall.

No one left the table, even though they'd all finished eating.

"Have you fed Melissa?" Jed finally asked.

Since the lasagna pan was empty, she guessed he was worried about that second helping he'd had. She raised one eyebrow. "I should hope so. Actually, I heated up a can of soup. She didn't want anything heavy." She frowned as she remembered how weak Melissa had seemed. She'd gotten sick so quickly. Last night she'd seemed fine.

"She'll be all right," Jed assured her, patting her hand.

Her eyes filled with tears that took her by surprise. "Thanks," she whispered, embarrassed.

"Well, since we're all waiting to hear about Abby's phone call, why don't we help Beth clean up," Jed said, standing.

Before she could protest, all the men were stacking dishes. Jed took over at the sink, rinsing the dishes, and Barney loaded the dishwasher. Dirk grabbed the broom and began sweeping the kitchen.

Floyd put away the condiments and butter and wiped down the cabinets and table.

Beth stared at them. Until Jed Davis arrived, the men had never offered to help. Now it was routine that they carried their dishes to the sink. But today, they were doing the entire job.

"Hey, maybe we don't need Ellen if you can cook as well as you clean," Abby suggested from the door.

Everyone in the room whirled around to stare at her, waiting for an explanation.

"Ellen said she'd love to come work for us. She'll be here in an hour." Abby turned to Beth. "So, she'll keep an eye on Melissa and prepare supper. You can have your lesson with Jed. And the rest of you can look forward to a good meal this evening."

Everyone cheered, then filed out the door, leaving a clean kitchen behind them.

Abby and Beth looked at each other in amazement.

"It was Jed's idea," Beth finally said.

"Incredible. I didn't think cowboys knew how to load a dishwasher."

They both chuckled, then grew serious.

"We should've thought about Ellen, checked on her, this past year."

"Yeah," Beth agreed. "She came over when Aunt Beulah got sick. I'm sorry we didn't realize she needed some help."

"Well, now we're the ones who need help. And she's going to save our bacon." Abby paused, then said, "I'm going to go see Melissa for a few minutes. Can you stay in until Ellen arrives? She asked us to call her Ellen, by the way. She's going to stay here. Put her in the back bedroom upstairs."

"Okay. I'd better put clean sheets on the bed and dust a little."

"Yeah," Abby agreed with a sigh. "Want some help?"

"No, go sit with Melissa. I don't have to clean the kitchen, so I can manage that."

Beth didn't get out of the house until almost three, time for her training. Ellen settled in right away, but she had some questions for Beth. And Ellen's coming would help Melissa get better since she had fully relaxed when she knew Ellen would be filling in for her.

"I was so worried," Melissa had said faintly. "I'm letting everyone down."

"Now, don't you worry about it, Melissa," Ellen had assured her. "I may not be a fancy cook, but I can put good food on the table. Did you eat lunch already?"

"Yes."

"Only a few sips of a can of soup," Beth corrected. "I couldn't get her to eat any more."

Ellen tsked, as Beth suddenly remembered her mother doing. "Child, that won't do. I'm going to make you some scrambled eggs. Then I'll be back up to feed you."

Melissa didn't bother protesting. "Can we keep her?" she asked after Ellen had left the room, as she'd once pleaded for a puppy.

Beth grinned. "I'm in favor of it."

When Beth left for the barn, she knew her sister would have excellent care, and a hot meal would be waiting when she finished her work.

She went first to the back corral, several carrots in her hand. She did as Jed had done, waiting patiently until the horse drew close enough to snatch a carrot. "You're a cautious horse, Mugsy. I wonder who named you? Maybe we should choose a new name. Something more romantic."

"How about Romeo?" a deep voice suggested.

She spun around, scaring the horse. "Quit sneaking up on me!"

"Guilty conscience?" Jed asked, raising one eyebrow.

"No! But I was concentrating."

"You're going to rename him?"

"Yes. And Romeo sounds like a good name."

Jed chuckled. "Seems kind of cruel to me. After all, he's a gelding. He won't be able to, uh, participate in any romance."

She raised her chin and looked down her nose at

him. "Seems appropriate to me. Romeo didn't do much participating, either."

"Ah. Okay, Romeo it is." He shoved back from the fence. "Ready to saddle up Shorty?"

"Yes," she said, her voice crisp. She wasn't going to be thought of as sappy and romantic.

"Good." He paused and cleared his throat. "I want to apologize for what I said last night. I was wrong to make light of your loss. It's just that—my experience was a lot different. I never stayed anywhere very long."

Beth's heart ached for the loneliness she heard in his voice. Before she could say anything, however, he added, "After last night's disaster, I think we'd do better if we stuck to business."

"Right," she agreed, a firm smile on her lips. Inside, however, she went into mourning. No more dances, no more strong arms around her, no more hoping for a killer kiss.

He strode ahead of her toward the barn without saying anything else. Her gaze focused on his tight jeans with a sigh. It was just as well. He would be moving on, and she wasn't going anywhere.

"You're pulling up in the saddle too soon in the turn," Jed explaining, frowning at Beth. They'd talked about the mechanics of the ride, but she still hadn't gotten it right to his satisfaction. "When you do that, it throws Shorty off."

"Okay. I'll try again."

They had been practicing twice a day for a week

now, since Ellen had moved to the ranch. A week since he'd suggested they stick to business. A week since Beth had smiled at him.

He wiped that thought from his head. Smiles didn't matter. She wanted to be the best barrel racer there was. That was all that mattered.

He watched her tug the hat down hard on her forehead, lean over Shorty, then jump-start him on the course. She raced around the barrels, making the loops, cutting close to the barrels. On the last one, her knee hit the barrel and knocked it over. She continued the race, zooming over the finish line, but disappointment rode her features.

"Did you hurt yourself?"

"Yes! No, it doesn't matter." She slid from the saddle and almost fell over. He grabbed her around the waist, feeling her curves against him for the first time since the dance. "Whoa, there, take it easy."

"I'm not a horse!" she protested.

"I never thought you were. Just a hardheaded woman."

She whirled around and shoved against his chest. "Get away. I need to walk it off before it stiffens up on me."

He stepped back a foot, close enough to catch her if she'd overestimated her strength, but far enough away that she could walk. When it appeared she could manage on her own, he trotted across the field to set up the barrel.

As he started back, he saw her swing up into the

saddle, but not with her usual style. "Wait!" he called.

She sat on her horse, not looking at him, a stubborn look on her face that he recognized.

"I'm a little tired," he said as he grew closer. "Why don't we call it a day?"

She didn't buy his attempt at subterfuge.

"No, thanks. You go on in. I'll practice a little longer."

"Beth, you're being stubborn. You've hurt your knee. There's no need to push things at this point. We've still got a couple of weeks before the rodeo in Ponca City."

He'd entered her at the first of the week, planning it to be her first test.

"Give me the stopwatch if you're going in."

"Damn it, woman, did you listen to anything I said?"

She stared at him. Short of hauling her off the horse and carrying her kicking and screaming into the house, he figured she was going to make another run.

"All right. Go when you're ready." With the stopwatch in hand, he watched her gather herself, then take off to ride the course again.

She and Shorty moved as one, rounding the first barrel. The barrel shivered as she made a tight turn, but it stayed upright. The turn on the second barrel was just as tight and Jed realized she was going to have a really good ride this time. Maybe good enough to satisfy her pride and let her quit a little early.

When she reached the third barrel, he noticed she seemed a little out of sync. Frowning, he watched as she came up out of the saddle before Shorty had completed the turn, throwing the horse off his stride.

Damn, she'd been doing so much better.

Then, as if in slow motion, she flew from the saddle and hit the ground, lying completely still.

Jed raced across the pasture, running faster than he'd ever done, fear driving him. "Beth! Beth, are you all right?"

Shorty had come to a halt nearby, looking puzzled, waiting for his rider.

She still hadn't moved.

Jed slid to his knees beside her, feeling for her pulse, wanting to snatch her up against him, to hold her close, but he was afraid to move her until he determined whether any bones were broken.

"Beth? Can you hear me, sweetheart?" He found a pulse and sighed in relief, but she appeared to have had the air knocked out of her. He tilted her head back and laid his mouth over hers, blowing air into her on a rhythmic beat.

When her arms came up around his neck and her lips moved under his, he knew she was awake. He knew she was safe, able to breathe on her own.

But, damn it, he couldn't turn her loose.

Instead, now that he knew she didn't have a broken bone, he pulled her body tightly against his and stroked her back, kissing her over and over again. Getting his fill of what he dreamed about each night.

Her hands held to his shoulders. Then fingers ran through his hair, traced his ear, then his muscles, but she never held back or pushed away.

Which probably explained why they were soon flat on the ground, him lying atop her, kissing her, stroking her, unbuttoning her shirt.

He wanted her so bad he figured he'd die if he didn't make love to her. The past week had been torture, trying to maintain that distance he'd told her they should keep. Now he was intent on touching every inch of her.

His tongue traced her full lips, persuading hers to do the same. Then he kissed her again and again, mating as surely as the even greater oneness he wanted to feel.

"Sweetheart," he panted, "are you all right?" Before she could answer, he kissed her again. Her shirt opened, revealing a lacy bra that covered her breasts, and his mouth moved to salute the mound of skin above the silk.

"Not out here," she moaned. "Someone will see." When she tried to pull her shirt back over that part of her body, he came to his senses.

"No! Not out here." He slowly rose to his feet, even though his body protested. "Beth, I'm—come on, I'll help you up."

"The barn. We can go to the barn," she said, her voice thin, as if she were having trouble getting her breath. She pushed herself up from the ground and reached for him as he tried to assist her.

Her mouth settled on his again before he could tell her he'd come to his senses. He intended to tell her that. Right away. But he had to kiss her first. She wanted him to.

When he realized what that line of reasoning was going to do to him, he pushed her away. "Beth! We can't—" He pulled her arms from around his neck. "Come on, sweetheart, let's get you to the house."

"Not the house," she muttered, and kissed him again, her hands pulling his shirt out of his jeans, then running up his chest underneath. He loved the feel of her hands on him.

He loved her mouth on his.

He loved—no, he couldn't do this! "Beth! Stop! We can't go any further."

When his words penetrated her head, she came to an abrupt halt. Her mouth withdrew, but her eyes were wide with shock as she stared at him. "What?"

"Beth, sweetheart, I can't make love to you. It wouldn't be right. You're my student. I'm only here for a little while. It would be wrong—"

Wrong, he thought, to lead an innocent like Beth on, but not fulfill the future she deserved. A house. A husband. Two things he could never give her.

Her hands slid out from his shirt and he felt the loss of her touch at once. He still had a hold of her shoulders, but she wrenched them from his hands and took several steps back.

"Look, Beth, I'm sorry. I was scared you were

hurt. I forgot myself. I lost control. You're a beautiful woman and it's hard—''

"You—you—lost control? So I was just a—a convenience? You thought you'd cop a feel since I was down on the ground anyway?'' The rising horror in her voice ripped at him.

"No! Not like that! Beth—'' He took a step toward her, wanting to ease her pain, reassure her.

She put out one hand and backed up. "Keep away from me. Don't even think about touching me.'' Then she spun on her heel and ran toward the house.

He considered running after her. But she was right. He couldn't touch her again. He'd backed away once, but he might not be strong enough again.

She was too tempting.

Shorty came over and nuzzled his shoulder.

He guessed he was the one to unsaddle her horse and rub him down tonight. A small price to pay for the big mistake he'd just made.

Chapter Nine

By the time Beth was halfway to the house, two things had happened. Her knee had really stiffened up on her. And her tears had been dried by her anger.

Damn the man! She had offered herself as a gift, and he'd thrown that gift back in her face. He didn't want her! Her rage built as her stomach churned with hurt. All week she'd tried to keep her mind on her training, on the ranch, on anything but Jed Davis.

Because he was right about one thing. There was no future for them. He would be moving on down the road. But every time she got near him, her body revved up, aching for his touch.

Even worse, her heart wanted to be near him, to watch his gentle caresses with the horses, his patience, his encouragement. He'd make a great daddy. She could just see him with a little boy, teaching him his cowboy ways.

The fact that the little boy was always her little boy, too, told her she was too far gone.

At night, she'd dreamed of him as a lover, strong but tender, encouraging, challenging, driving her wild with his touch. And she'd been right.

Today he'd proved that as a lover, he'd be in big demand. If the women around here had experienced what she had today, they'd be lined up all the way to Oklahoma.

But he wouldn't make love to her. She was his student. Maybe he should call Sissy Stallings when he got an urge! That thought had her almost biting a hole through her bottom lip. She'd kill both of them!

Ellen must have seen her coming because she stepped out on the back porch. "You okay, hon?"

"I hurt my knee," Beth replied, unwilling to speak about what had really upset her.

"Is it swollen?"

"Yeah, I think so. I'm going to go soak it in the tub, Ellen. I hope you don't mind if I miss dinner tonight."

"Don't be silly, child. After you soak it, slip into bed, and I'll bring you some dinner upstairs." Ellen smiled, as if Beth's behavior was normal.

With a grateful smile, Beth eased her way up the steps and into the house. At least she didn't have to face Jed tonight. She'd worry about the training in the morning.

Ellen watched as Beth hurried past her. She'd been crying. Not now. But the tear tracks down her cheeks, through the fine layer of dust, were still there.

Turning to stare out at the pasture where Beth and Jed Davis did their training, Ellen wondered. She didn't think a bum knee would cause that many tears. Beth Kennedy was no wimp.

No, the only thing that caused a woman that many tears was a man.

When Abby came in, a few minutes before the cowboys were called to dinner, Ellen stopped her. "Beth got hurt this afternoon. Banged up her knee. She's not coming down to supper."

It was the last sentence that got Abby's attention, bringing her to an abrupt halt. "Not coming down to dinner? Is she hurt that bad?"

Ellen slowly turned around. "I don't like to butt in."

Abby stared at her, then nodded. "Butt away. You're part of us now."

"It'd be my guess that she and Mr. Davis had a, uh, a disagreement."

With a nod, Abby patted Ellen on the shoulder. "Thanks. I'll go talk to her."

When Ellen sounded the dinner bell, Abby returned to the kitchen. "You're right, but she's not talking."

Ellen wasn't surprised. "Let's see if Mr. Davis comes to dinner."

He did, but he was the last to enter the kitchen and he made an immediate inventory of the occupants. Abby and Ellen exchanged a glance, but neither said anything.

Ellen had been busy all afternoon, and she served her special meatloaf, with fresh steamed vegetables and hot biscuits. The appreciative murmurs from the men, especially Floyd, made her feel wonderful. She loved being part of a family again.

She wondered how long Jed would hold out before he asked the question she knew was driving him crazy. He lasted about three minutes, just enough time to fill his plate.

But the hungry cowboy hadn't taken a bite.

"Where's Beth?"

Ellen passed the biscuits to Barney, avoiding Jed's stare.

Abby had a bite of meatloaf on the way to her mouth, but she paused. "Her knee was still hurting her, so she's soaking it."

"She get hurt?" Barney asked, concern in his voice.

Abby explained about Beth's knocking over the barrel with her knee.

Before she'd finished, Jed had come to his feet. "Maybe I should go check on her."

Abby laughed. "I don't think she's dressed for company, cowboy. She's in the tub."

Everyone laughed except for Jed, whose cheeks burned. "When she gets out of the tub, I mean. I've had a lot of experience—" his face actually got redder, to Ellen's fascination "—with injuries, I mean."

Her motherly instincts on high alert, Ellen could stand it no longer. Gently she said, "Sit down and eat your dinner, Jed. You've put in a long day. We're taking care of Beth.''

He looked so lost she wanted to put an arm around him, but she knew better.

Dirk, the least talkative of the cowboys, must have sensed something, because he initiated conversation. ''That horse, the Stallings horse, I think he's settling down.''

Jed slumped into his chair, a frown on his face. ''Uh, yeah, a little.''

''What's his name?'' Dirk persisted.

''It was Mugsy,'' Jed said. Then a small smile played on his lips. ''But Beth renamed him. She wants to call him Romeo.''

Floyd reared back. ''She wants to call a gelding Romeo?''

Jed shrugged. ''It's her horse.''

Ellen looked at Abby again as silence fell, the men eating their meal. Abby, too, was eating. She worked as hard as any of the men. But, also, she was keeping an eye on Jed.

If Ellen hadn't been told by the other men that her meatloaf was wonderful, she might have gotten a complex. Jed was stirring his food but eating very little of it.

''Aren't you hungry, pal?'' Floyd asked.

Jed gave a start and quickly looked around the table. Then he loaded a big bite on his fork. ''Sure. I just didn't want to wolf mine down like you hungry galoots. What will Ellen think?''

He even managed a smile, but Ellen wasn't fooled. She smiled in return and was grateful a lovesick cowboy was incapable of reading anyone's mind.

When Jed had forced in all the food he could stomach, afraid he wouldn't be able to keep down any of it, he gathered his plate and carried it to the sink before anyone could see how little he'd eaten.

"That was mighty fine, Miss Ellen. You're a great cook," he said, managing a smile as he turned back to the table. "I'll help Miss Ellen with the dishes, Miss Abby, if you want to check on Beth. I mean, Miss Beth. Then, you know, if you need me to look at her knee, I can—well, check it out."

Abby smiled at him, making him feel lower than a snake's belly. If she knew what he'd done to her baby sister today, she'd take a whip to him.

"I think what we need to do is quit being so formal. Just call me Abby, Jed. You're right, I'd better go check on Beth, and Melissa, too, but I'm sure she's fine. Then I'll help Ellen with the dishes."

"All these offers to help are nice, but cleaning up is my job. I can manage." Ellen stood and began clearing the table.

Floyd jumped to his feet and began helping. Barney and Dirk followed him.

"Now, wait just a minute," Ellen protested. "I spent half the afternoon making apple pie. I expect everyone to eat at least one slice, so just sit yourselves back down."

Delight spread over Floyd, Barney and Dirk's

faces and they immediately returned to the table. Jed apparently hadn't even heard her, since he remained standing at the cabinet.

Abby smiled at Ellen. "I'll go check on Melissa and Beth and then have my piece."

Jed released the breath he'd been holding and took a step toward the door where Abby disappeared.

Ellen took hold of his shoulders. "Back to the table, cowboy. I'm serving pie."

He frowned. "Uh, no, I don't—I'm not hungry."

"It will give you something to do until Abby comes back," Ellen whispered.

Jed whipped around to stare at the woman. Had Beth told her? His heart settled back into place. No, Beth hadn't said anything. Otherwise, neither Abby nor Ellen would have smiled at him.

With an abrupt nod, he sat back down.

Beth had stayed in the tub until after dinner began downstairs. Then she'd gotten out, dressed in her pajamas and old terry-cloth robe and hobbled into Melissa's room.

"How you doing, sis?" she asked.

"Better than you, from what I hear," Melissa said softly.

She still sounded weak to Beth. Worry filled her. Melissa's health was a lot more important than her love life.

Ha! What love life?

She pulled a chair up to the bed and sat down, propping her leg on the mattress. "Abby told you?"

"Yeah, how's the knee?"

She made light of her injury and spent the next half hour trying to think of humorous things to cheer up Melissa. But it wasn't easy. Her mind stayed on what had happened in the pasture and the sexy cowboy downstairs.

In the middle of a story that wasn't very funny, the door opened and Abby strolled in.

"Dinner over?" Beth asked, wanting to know if Jed had actually appeared. It had occurred to her a few minutes ago that he might have been a no-show like her.

"All except for the apple pie," Abby assured her with a smile. To Melissa, she said, "The guys said to get well soon, but now that Ellen's in the kitchen, they're not in a panic. Hope that doesn't hurt your feelings."

Melissa grinned. "Nope. I'm thinking we might not want to ever let her go."

Abby and Melissa smiled and Beth tried to join in, but she was busy trying to figure out how to ask about Jed.

Abby saved her the trouble. "Jed wants to know how's your knee."

Beth's head jerked up and she stared at her sister.

"He's offered to look at it. Says he can tell if you need a doctor to examine it."

The thought of Jed Davis touching her, even just for medical purposes, was enough to drive her crazy. She wanted him to make love to her, not play Dr. Kildare.

She tried a casual laugh. "You know me, Abby. I'd tell you if it was anything serious. I'll be fine by the morning."

"Sure," Abby said. "But you did miss dinner. That's not like you."

"Ellen said she'd bring me something up. I hope there are some leftovers."

"I think she put food back for both of you before we started, just to be on the safe side." Abby walked over to the window that looked out on the barns. "Anything go wrong today?"

"You've already asked me that," Beth reminded her.

Abby turned around to stare at her. "Oh, yeah. And you told me you banged your knee. Anything else go wrong?"

With both her sisters staring at her, Beth couldn't tell a complete lie. She licked her lips as she constructed her answer. "Jed got bossy. I lost my temper. He lost his."

Simple. That's what she'd always heard about lying. Keep it simple. Too many details always gave the liar away.

Abby grinned. "I can't say I'm surprised. You two seem to have something going."

"What do you mean?" Beth asked with a gasp.

Abby shrugged her shoulders. "I'm not sure. But last Friday night, I thought the room might catch on fire whenever the two of you danced."

"Abby!" Beth protested.

"Beth!" Abby returned, grinning even more.

Beth turned away, unable to meet Abby's look when she felt like crying.

After a minute, Abby said, "So, you want him to look at the knee?"

"No!"

"You want to tell him anything?"

Oh, yeah. She wanted to tell the jerk to go to hell! As if her knee was the problem! "No."

"Do you owe him an apology? Or he you?" Abby's tone was more serious now.

She fought the tears that wanted out. "No," she whispered. "No. It was just a difference of opinion."

She wanted him. He didn't want her.

Keeping her gaze locked on her hands, she waited for Abby's response. She loved her sisters. She'd always told them everything. Maybe it was a sign of growing up that she couldn't talk now.

Or maybe it was because she'd screwed up bigtime.

When Abby came back into the kitchen, Jed was on his feet before she could reach the table.

"Beth?" he questioned, his gaze fixed on Abby's face.

"She's doing fine," Abby said, a smile on her lips. "I don't think we'll need the doctor."

"Maybe I should look at it anyway."

"Beth's pretty good at letting us know when she's hurt." Abby sat down at the table. "Any apple pie left, Ellen?"

Jed stood there, trying to think of another way to

see Beth. He had to see her, to be sure she—she what? She forgave him? She'd ever speak to him again? She wasn't firing him on the spot?

"Sit down, Jed," Abby ordered softly.

He fell into the chair and clenched his hands together on the table.

"Look, quit worrying. Beth told me."

Jed thought he was having a heart attack. His mouth hung open and he stared at Abby. "She told you?" he finally got out, though his voice sounded as though he was choking.

Abby laughed, and Jed stared at her as if she were crazy.

"Shoot, Jed, it's not the first time Beth has lost her temper. And I think I can forgive you for losing yours. I've been on the receiving end of Beth's anger. She can get under your skin, can't she?"

He couldn't speak, so he nodded. Oh, yeah, she could get under his skin. She could completely fill him with such need, he wasn't sure he could survive without her.

Floyd was the only cowboy left in the kitchen. He and Ellen had been finishing up the dishes. Now he stepped closer to the table. "Miss Abby, I can promise you that Jed's a good man."

"I know, Floyd."

Ellen set a piece of pie in front of Abby. "I'm going to take food up to the girls."

Jed leaped to his feet again. "I'll carry the tray. It, uh, it might be heavy."

Abby turned to look at Ellen, and he didn't know

what she was thinking, but he was relieved when she nodded. "That's real thoughtful of you, Jed. They're both in Melissa's room, Ellen."

"I can help, too," Floyd offered.

"No!" Jed ordered loudly, then dropped his gaze. He hadn't meant to sound so desperate.

Abby was still smiling. She looked at Floyd. "Why don't you finish your coffee and keep me company while I have my pie," she suggested to Floyd.

"I'll even cut you another piece, if you want, Floyd," Ellen offered.

Jed looked at the woman and then Floyd, surprised to see such warmth in their gazes. What the hell was Floyd up to?

"Yes, ma'am, I'd like that just fine." He sat back down at the table.

Jed stood there while Ellen cut another piece of pie and took it to Floyd. Then she added a couple more things to the tray. "Okay, Jed, it's ready. I'll show you the way."

He lifted the tray and followed Ellen from the room, each step taking him closer to Beth.

"You okay?" Melissa asked softly.

Beth nodded. "Yeah, but you don't need all this. I'm going to my room."

"But supper," Melissa protested.

Beth felt like a bad person, disturbing Melissa when she was so sick. She touched her sister's hand and swung her bum leg to the floor. "I'm not hungry.

You eat my share and then get some rest. I'll check on you in the morning.''

She hobbled down the hall to her room, across from the room Ellen was using. Just as she entered her room, she heard footsteps on the stairs. Good. She thought Melissa could use some soothing company. Either Abby or Ellen would be better for Melissa than she would.

And she had a lot of thinking to do.

Like what she was going to do tomorrow.

Her anger had faded. Now all she felt was shame. She'd thrown herself at Jed. He'd been giving her mouth-to-mouth, trying to help her. And she'd latched on to him and wouldn't let go.

Then, when he'd expressed his disinterest, she'd acted as if he'd led her on.

The man had asked for her to stick to business. He was probably packing his bags right now. He'd load up his horses and be on the road by sunup. Gone.

Out of her life.

Her eyes filled with tears again.

Jed stood clutching the tray as Ellen rapped softly on the closed door. When he heard a soft request to enter, his heart began racing even faster.

Ellen opened the door and he followed on her heels. Immediately, he scanned the room. The only occupant was a pale Melissa, sitting up in the bed.

''Where's Beth?'' he demanded, staring at her sister.

Melissa seemed taken aback by his brusqueness.

"Easy, Jed," Ellen whispered.

"Sorry. I—I'm concerned about her knee." That damn knee was taking on epic proportions.

"It's a little stiff," Melissa assured him.

"Is she feeling worse?"

"I don't think so. But she said she really wasn't hungry, Ellen. Sorry."

"Land's sake, Melissa, I'm not offended, but I do worry about her not eating. She worked hard today, too," Ellen said.

"Maybe I should go see if she's changed her mind," Jed suggested, trying to sound offhand.

"I don't think—" Melissa began.

"But she should eat something," Ellen insisted. "Maybe you could just knock on her door and ask," she added, looking at Jed.

"Yeah, I'll do that. Uh, which room is hers?"

"Jed, she's—she's not feeling well. She may need a little time to recover," Melissa said gently.

"I won't push her, Melissa, I promise." He tried a smile, but he didn't think he was very successful. "But I'm worried she's not taking care of herself."

"Go on, Jed. Ask her. She's in the last room on the left." Ellen began setting Melissa's food on the bedside table. "Tell her I can bring her food to her, if she wants."

"Okay." He slipped from the room and practically ran down the hall. When he reached the last door, he rapped on it.

"Who is it?"

He took a deep breath. "It's Jed."

Chapter Ten

Beth almost fell out of the bed. She stood and took a step toward the door.

Jed? Jed was knocking on her bedroom door? She couldn't think of any reason for his presence.

"Beth? Dinner's ready."

She hadn't imagined it. That was definitely Jed's voice. Sinking onto the edge of her bed, she stared at the wooden panels that separated her from the sexy, infuriating cowboy. "I—I'm not hungry."

Silence. Had he gone away?

"I think you should eat."

"No. Go away, Jed." There. She'd ended it. He'd go now.

"Beth, I'm worried about you."

Worried about her? How dare he! It was his fault! Then honesty forced her to admit it was her fault.

She'd been the one to change the lifesaving to kissing. A small sob escaped her.

"Beth?"

"I'm fine. Go away."

"Beth, sweetheart, I can't—"

That endearment, coming from his lips, set off her anger all over again. Before he could finish his sentence, she'd sprung from her bed and raced to the door. Yanking it open, she whispered, "Don't call me that!"

"What? What did I—"

"Sweetheart! You called me sweetheart! Don't do that again!" She sounded completely crazy, she realized. The man was going to think she'd lost her mind. She attempted to slam the door, but a cowboy boot was in the way.

"Go away!" she repeated.

"Are you all right? Does your knee hurt?"

"Yes, my knee hurts." She glared at him, unable to understand why she was having to have this conversation.

"I'm sorry," he whispered.

She knew he wasn't referring to her knee. His blue eyes looked somber, filled with regret. Suddenly all the anger went out of her and she wanted to cry again.

But not in front of Jed Davis.

"Forget about it."

"Beth, do you want me to leave?"

Her heart constricted. Want him to leave? Never. But what would be best? She looked at him and couldn't say the words. Shaking her head no, she finally whispered, "Not unless you want to. I'll understand if you want to back out."

"We've got enough time before the Ponca City rodeo. I think we can make some improvements if we keep working."

She held back a groan of frustration. She wanted to jump the man's bones, and all he could think about was a barrel race. "Yeah, fine. But I may not ride in the morning."

"Okay, sure. Take the whole day off. We'll start again after that. And I'll tell Ellen to bring your dinner."

After he withdrew his boot, she closed the door and started back to the bed. She passed by the dresser mirror and almost died of embarrassment.

No wonder Jed hadn't wanted her.

She was wearing old flannel pajamas, her hair was wild, and her nose from red from crying. Oh, yeah. She really knew how to attract a man.

She fell facedown on her bed, tears seeping out of her eyes, her misery complete.

Two days later, everything was normal again.

Unless one counted the fact that Jed never spoke.

Beth never smiled.

And everyone tiptoed around them.

But she was training again, twice a day. She and Shorty ran the course over and over again. And her time was improving. According to Jed, she was a shoo-in for first place.

That was one of two comments he'd made. The other one was "Good job."

The rest of the time, he watched her like a hawk. And kept a good ten yards' distance between them. As if he was afraid she'd kiss him again.

She supposed she should be grateful he made it impossible for her to make a fool of herself. Because she still longed for his touch. She still waited for his smile, that sexy grin that made her want to do anything he asked.

Most of all, she waited for him to call her sweetheart.

He didn't do any of those things. He worked hard, all day long. He skipped lunch a couple of days, until Ellen started fixing him a pack of food. He picked at his food at breakfast and dinner, sitting at the opposite end of the table from her.

In fact, Ellen said something about him losing weight. And she was right. Beth knew things couldn't go on much longer the way they were. She figured Jed would stay until the Ponca City rodeo and then he'd leave.

When Saturday night came, Beth had suffered about as much as she could suffer. She blamed herself for everything going wrong. She didn't know much about men. Aunt Beulah had taught her a lot but not on that subject. So she supposed she'd handled everything wrong. But knowing that didn't help make things right.

She decided the first thing to do was get her mind off Jed. And the only way to do that was to find another man. Someone who might be interested in her. And to do that, she'd have to leave the ranch.

She rapped on Abby's door. She'd come in a few minutes ago to clean up for dinner.

"Yes?"

Beth opened the door. "You want to go into town tonight?"

Abby frowned. "Into town? You mean, to Casey's?" Casey's was the local bar and grill in Tumbleweed, the closest town, where most of the younger set hung out.

"Yeah. I've got a case of cabin fever."

"Oh, Beth, that would be good for you, but I can't go. I promised myself I'd do the tax work. Quarterly payments are due day after tomorrow. Look, how about we go after I get the taxes done. It will just be a couple of days."

Beth looked away, afraid Abby would see too much. "Don't worry about it. Can I help?"

"No, I'm afraid not."

"Okay, I'll call a friend to meet me there. So I won't be at dinner."

"I don't like you going alone," Abby protested.

With a wry smile, Beth said, "I'm a big girl, Abby. I'll be careful."

Abby crossed the room and hugged Beth, almost bringing tears to her eyes. "You take care now, you hear?"

"I will. And I won't stay out too late."

She kissed her sister's cheek and scooted out of the room before Abby could come up with a reason for her to stay home. She couldn't do that. She had to get her mind off Jed Davis.

She hurried down the stairs and out of the house. Her truck was parked nearby and she slipped behind the wheel and started the motor. As she was backing out, Ellen came onto the porch to ring the supper bell.

Jed came through the kitchen door last, as he always did these days, but his gaze immediately searched for Beth. She wasn't down yet.

He settled into the seat by Ellen, the one he'd adopted as his own because Beth always sat at the opposite end of the table, next to Abby.

This way he could see her, but he couldn't even think of touching her. Or even pick up her scent, which haunted him every night when he tried to sleep.

"Jed, you're lookin' mighty tired," Floyd commented, sitting down across from him. He never wavered on his seat choice, either. He stayed next to Ellen, too.

"Didn't sleep good last night," Jed muttered.

"Are you not feeling well?" Ellen asked as she joined them at the table, having put several serving platters on the table.

Jed smiled. The woman was a born mother, even though she'd never had kids. "I'm fine." Better than fine since he heard footsteps on the stairs. He gazed at the kitchen door, waiting for Beth to come in.

It was Abby.

She took her place at the head of the table, asked the blessing and began passing platters.

An uneasy feeling filled him.

"Where's Beth?" he asked, watching her sister's face.

"She's gone out for the evening. And Melissa still isn't ready to come to dinner. But she's doing much better, don't you think, Ellen?"

Ellen agreed.

Jed didn't care about Melissa. Oh, he did, of course, but Melissa wasn't the one driving him crazy.

"She go out alone?"

Everyone stared at him. Okay, it wasn't his business, but he had to know.

Abby's eyebrows rose, but she answered him. "She said she was going to meet some friends at Casey's, the local hangout in town."

"Isn't it dangerous for her to go alone? I mean, sometimes, maybe, there are some rough characters in those places."

Abby smiled. "She promised she'd be careful."

He couldn't ask any more questions. He'd already exceeded politeness. Forcing himself to eat a reasonable amount of dinner so he wouldn't call attention to himself, he made his way through the meal.

When he could leave the table with the rest of the men, he looked at Floyd. "Want to go into town? Look around?"

Floyd seemed embarrassed. "Well, actually, I'm taking Ellen into town. There's a movie playing we wanted to see."

Ellen coughed. Floyd didn't look happy. It took Jed a minute to figure out what was happening, until Floyd said, "You could come with us...if you want to."

Okay, so now he got it. Floyd had a date and he was afraid Jed would horn in on it.

"Thanks, but I'm not much on movies. I'll see you later." Jed then hurried out of the house, straight to his pickup.

He wasn't interested in movie stars. His attention was focused on Beth Kennedy, his own personal siren. He had to make sure she was okay.

A few minutes later, he pulled into the parking lot at Casey's, not surprised to find it full of pickup trucks. Cowboys played as hard as they worked. And Saturday night was their night to let it all hang out.

He was relieved to see the truck Beth usually drove parked a row over. At least he'd found her. But what if he walked in to find her in the arms of another man? What if she was snuggled up tight to some big old cowboy, letting him touch her?

Damn, it was going to be a long night.

He headed for the front door.

Beth checked her watch. She'd only been here an hour. It had seemed like seven days.

There was a lot of drinking and smoking going on. Some flirting, some dancing, some necking. In the darker corners, more serious stuff could be taking place.

She didn't care. Oh, she'd danced a little. Talked

a little. Drunk a little ginger ale. She wasn't about to drink beer when she was on her own, and had to drive home. Aunt Beulah had taught her better than that.

And so far, she'd accomplished absolutely nothing. No one there had perfect blue eyes, broad shoulders, his sexy grin, his gentle touch. A gentle touch. A sexy grin. She wasn't going to think about Jed Davis. She wasn't.

"Want to dance, darlin'?"

She looked up to find another cowboy at her elbow. He seemed okay, mostly sober. With a shrug of her shoulders, she decided she'd give it one more try, and then call it a night.

"Sure." Sliding off the stool, she led the way to the small dance floor.

Immediately she knew she'd made a mistake. The man plastered himself all over her, his hands immediately sliding down to cup her hips. She grabbed both his hands and shoved them up to her waist, then pushed against his chest.

"I like to breathe while I dance, cowboy," she said firmly, "and keep your hands above the waist."

"Yes, ma'am," he said with a grin.

His hand immediately rose toward her breasts.

"I'm going to knee you from here to the Canadian border if you even try it."

"Well, now, honey, I just wanted to warm you up." His lopsided grin told her she might have misjudged his sobriety.

"I have to go," she said abruptly, and pulled out

of his hold. She wasn't going to be mauled by some drunk.

"Hey, I'll be good. I promise. Just finish the dance. Otherwise, I'll look like a fool standing here by myself."

His plaintive words stopped her. It would embarrass him for her to walk off in the middle of a dance. As long as he behaved, she could finish the song.

With a nod, she put one hand on his shoulder and took his other hand in hers. "As long as you behave."

"Yes, ma'am."

She didn't relax, which was a good thing, since he scooted a little closer with each note of the song. When his left hand began to slip a little, she came to an abrupt halt. It immediately returned to her waist.

"You're a hardhearted woman," he complained. Then, as if he thought it seductive, he began an off-key humming that seldom connected with the tune being sung.

It was the dance from hell.

It had nothing in common with her dances with Jed. She closed her eyes, remembering those stolen moments when his strength had protected her, his warmth had seduced her, as they'd moved around the floor.

The music ended, awakening her from her memories. She stepped away from her partner.

"Hey, don't go. They're gonna play another one," he said, reaching for her.

"Thanks, but I have to go. It's late."

"Lady, the sun's hardly down. It's not even nine o'clock. Even damn old Cinderella didn't have to be home till midnight."

She glared at him and walked around him. Her keys, license and money were in her pockets, so she didn't even need to go back to the table she'd occupied. With a wave to a couple of friends she saw across the room, she headed for the door.

This had been a dumb idea. As though another man could distract her from what she was feeling for Jed Davis. It would take longer than one evening to get the man out of her head.

It might take forever.

Jed had found a table in the dim corner of the bar, not close to where Beth was sitting. She stayed at the table alone, for a few minutes. Then that cowboy had led her out onto the dance floor.

He'd gritted his teeth as the man pulled her too close. Beth had taken care of that business, though. A grin cracked his grim mask. She was pretty good at taking care of herself.

But he hated watching her with another man. Any man. He had it bad. The past few nights, he'd been thinking. He'd figured his fascination with Beth Kennedy would wear off. He'd never found a woman more important than his plans.

Until now.

He was beginning to wonder if he could ever forget her. If his dreams would have any meaning without Beth in them. If he could walk away.

He was too old for her, of course. He'd found out she was only twenty-five. He was thirty-two. He felt older.

She had more money than he did. But he wasn't poor. He'd built his savings up so he could soon buy his dream, a home, a ranch. And he had skills that would enhance any operation.

Damn it! What was the problem? Why couldn't he have Beth? Maybe he wasn't good enough for her. Maybe he'd never be good enough for her.

Maybe he didn't know about families. That's why he thought he'd be better off alone. But not now. He didn't think he could live without Beth. If he explained—he didn't want to do that. He didn't like talking about his childhood.

The old feeling that it was somehow his fault, that he was unlovable, rose up in him. He'd shut those feelings away, until now. Would Beth reject him when she found out? Would she believe he couldn't be a good husband because he didn't know about families?

He slammed his fist on the table, drawing the attention of those around him. He had to try. He couldn't stand back and watch someone else take her sweetness, her beauty, her loyalty and hard work.

He was the one who'd make her happy.

He stood, ready to go tell her, when he realized she'd left the dance floor and was heading out the door. He threw a couple of dollars down on the table to pay for the Coke he'd been drinking.

That was a real sign he was a goner. He wouldn't take the chance of drinking tonight. She might need him.

Glad he knew where she was parked, he came out into the darkness and turned right. This parking lot needed better lights. It had been dusk when he'd arrived. He hadn't realized there was only one light, over the front door.

When he got to Beth's truck, he realized it was empty.

Frowning, he looked around, but he didn't see her. He knew she'd come outside. Where had she gone?

When he heard a scream, he knew instantly it was Beth and he sped in the direction from which it had come.

Beth hadn't realized her last dance partner had followed her from the bar until he grabbed hold of her as she stepped out of the small circle of light.

"Turn me loose," she ordered, trying to sound firm.

"I will, darlin', I will, just as soon as you give me a little kiss."

She protested, but he dragged her along. He was a big man, with hard muscles, and she couldn't break free, or get in a position to fight back, since he kept her off balance.

"Stop! I don't want—"

He pulled her against him and covered her mouth

with his. She was disgusted. He tasted of stale liquor and cigarette smoke. She pushed against him, trying to break his hold. As soon as he lifted his mouth, she screamed at the top of her lungs, figuring she wouldn't have much time to summon help. Though she doubted anyone would hear over the music.

"Be quiet!"

She wasn't about to follow those orders. She screamed again.

He raised his hand to deliver a blow, and she tried to get her knee up.

Then, suddenly, she was free. A dark shadow had grabbed the man from behind and spun him around.

"Say good-night, cowboy," a deep voice ordered, and she knew who her savior was. Jed Davis to the rescue.

His fist pounded into the cowboy's chin and he fell to the ground, a suddenly silent sack of a man.

"You okay?" Jed asked, reaching for her.

There was no hesitation on her part. She flung herself into his arms. "Jed!" she cried, wishing she could erase the memory of that wretched kiss with a heavenly one from him.

But even in the shock of the moment, she didn't forget that he didn't want her. So she hugged him, then backed away. "I'm fine."

"Did he hurt you?"

"He—he grabbed me, but—"

"Damn!" Jed muttered, and whirled around, seized the man by the collar of his shirt and hauled him to his feet as he was coming to.

"I don't know where you're from, but that's not how you treat women in Texas," Jed explained. Then he struck two more blows, one in the stomach and another at the chin.

The cowboy staggered back.

Beth grabbed Jed's arm. "Please, Jed, can we go home? I want to go home."

"Yeah, sweetheart, I'll take you home."

"What about him?"

Jed turned to stare again at the man sitting on the gravel parking lot. "What about him? You want to press charges?"

"No. But I guess I should."

Jed hauled the man to his feet again. "Show me some ID."

"I'm not showing you anything," the man muttered, trying to free himself.

Over his shoulder, Jed said, "Go tell the bartender to call the police. We'll at least let them know what kind of bastard they've got hanging around here."

She hurried away.

"Come on, man, let me go," the cowboy whined. "She led me on, let me think she wanted me. So I misjudged the situation. That's not a hanging offense."

Jed couldn't believe the man's stupidity. "You say one more word about the lady, and you're going back down. I watched you manhandle her on the dance floor. She wasn't encouraging you."

"Hell, she shouldn't have such a tight little body

if she doesn't want us sniffing around her. I could—''

Jed hit him again.

He'd warned him.

Chapter Eleven

Beth came hurrying back out of Casey's. "What happened?"

"Nothing. I think he tripped," Jed said, giving her a brief smile. "Did the bartender call the police?"

"Yes. He didn't want to, but I persuaded him."

Jed's smile widened. "I won't even ask how."

The man on the ground attempted to get to his feet, but Jed nudged him with his boot. "Just stay down there. It'll save you some bruises."

"Hey, I'm leaving. And you're not going to stop me." He scrambled to his feet, as far from Jed as he could get.

Jed shook his head in disgust. "I told you to stay put." Then he grabbed him by his shirtfront and slammed him up against the nearest pickup. About that time, he heard the sirens in the distance.

"Go over there to the light so they can see you,

sweetheart," he ordered. "Then bring them over here."

As soon as Beth left, the cowboy tried to swing a punch at Jed. With his left fist, Jed doubled the man over with a powerful punch to his stomach. "You are one stubborn cowpoke. All you're doing is hurting yourself.

The man remained slumped over until the policeman, led by Beth, got there.

"What's going on here?"

Jed shoved the cowboy toward the cop. "We'll talk as soon as you cuff him. He keeps thinking he's going somewhere."

The officer frowned, but he quickly cuffed the man. "Okay, someone explain."

"You didn't tell him?" Jed asked Beth. He noted she was looking a little stubborn herself.

"Oh, I told him. He insisted I probably flirted too much." Beth turned to glare at the officer.

"Damn, you haven't had your sensitivity training yet, have you?" Jed stepped closer. "Look, the cowboy asked her to dance. I watched them. He kept overstepping the mark, she kept pushing him away. She left alone. He followed."

"Why were you watching her?"

Jed's gaze met briefly with Beth's, then he looked back at the cop. "Because I know her and I got worried when I saw how this man was treating her. When I saw her leave, I paid my bill and came after her to be sure she was all right. This skunk was close behind her, however, and dragged her off into the shadows.''

The officer turned to Beth. ''What did he do to you?''

''He—he kissed me. I tried to fight him but he's too big. When he took his mouth off me, I screamed. Then he told me to be quiet, so I screamed again. He was going to hit me when Jed came.''

''Okay, we'll book him on assault.''

''Hey,'' the cowboy protested. ''He hit me. Book him, too.''

The officer shook his head. ''I think that was justified. You got any ID?''

They discovered a few minutes later why the man hadn't wanted to show any identification. There were several warrants out for his arrest. One for rape, another for assault.

Jed and Beth were free to go. He took her arm and started toward his pickup.

''I'm parked over there,'' Beth said.

''I know, but we'll come back and get your truck tomorrow.'' He wanted her close to him. He wanted to tell her about his revelation, that maybe they were meant for each other. That he'd been wrong when he'd refused to make love to her.

''No, I'll take my truck. You can follow me.''

He frowned at her and she added, ''If you're going home now.''

''Of course I'm going home now.''

He'd only come into the damn town to see about her. ''Look, sweetheart—''

"You promised you wouldn't call me that."

Her angry tone, as well as the words, brought him to an abrupt halt. Did she hate him? "You didn't object when that gorilla was mauling you."

She ducked her head. "I know, and I'm grateful for your help. But that doesn't change anything."

She didn't care about him. She might have had the hots for him one day, but she didn't care about him. What he'd imagined she'd been feeling wasn't true.

His features hardened and he glared at her. "Fine. I'll follow you home." He stared at her, waiting for her response. She glanced at him, then turned away and hurried to her pickup.

"Damn, damn, damn!" he growled as he slid into his truck, slamming the door behind him.

What a hell of a night.

Beth didn't want to talk to Jed again that night. But when she got out of her pickup, she didn't have a choice. Hurrying over to his truck, she waited until he'd closed the door.

"Yeah?" he growled, staring at her.

Well, she'd gotten her wish. He wasn't calling her sweetheart now.

"I need to ask a favor."

He stood there, his hands resting on his hips, his handsome face hard as a rock. "What?"

"Don't tell Abby what happened."

She held her breath, waiting for his response.

"Why?"

"Because it will make her worry. She's got

enough to deal with, with Melissa sick. I'll be more careful in the future, I promise.''

He reached out a hand and Beth held her breath, thinking he meant to touch her. But he dropped his hand and turned away. "Okay," he muttered, "I won't say anything."

"Thank you," she returned, but she thought her heart was breaking. The man must hate her. He might have called her sweetheart in the heat of the moment, but he had no interest in her now.

Just like he might have wanted her for sex when she kissed him a million times, but he didn't want anything serious.

She guessed she owed him, because she was sure learning about men and—and sex…the hard way. Learning about hunger, about need…about heartache.

She turned and ran for the security of the house.

The next morning, Beth joined Abby in church. Ellen stayed home to take care of Melissa, though she usually attended.

"It was nice of Ellen to offer to stay home," Beth said.

"Yeah. We're going to take turns. Next week is mine, and the week after will be yours." Abby was reading the church bulletin.

"Good. 'Cause next Saturday is the Ponca City rodeo. So I'll be free the next weekend."

Abby looked up. "I'd forgotten Jed entered you

in that rodeo. It will be your first competition. Melissa will hate to miss it.''

Beth beat back the tears. Did she have to cry at everything these days? "Yeah, I'll miss both of you being there to root me on.''

"Hey, I'll be there. I can make it a day trip and be back by nightfall.''

"Oh, Abby, you have so much to do, I can't ask—''

Her sister grinned. "You're not asking. And you're not big enough to keep me away.''

Beth squeezed her sister's hand in gratitude. The start of the organ music warned them the service was about to begin and they fell silent.

During the sermon, which Beth scarcely heard, she thought about how important her sisters were to her life. That was a gift from Aunt Beulah. The social services representative had intended to put them in separate homes. That would have changed their lives forever.

Instead, Aunt Beulah had opened her home and her arms for them, and they'd remained a close-knit family.

Jed had been alone. He must have been so frightened, moving from place to place, never belonging. Maybe that was why he never settled down now. He was used to moving on.

Could any woman ever persuade him a home was more important than the next ranch...or woman...over the hill?

The thought of Jed with another woman, any

woman, brought a shaft of pain that made her gasp, drawing Abby's gaze.

Leaning over, Abby whispered, ''You okay?''

Beth nodded and avoided her gaze.

Then she thought about her time with Jed Davis. Had she tried to convince him? Had she tried to make him fall in love with her? Or had she tried to seduce him? Maybe she needed to work harder at showing him she was a mature, hard worker. Maybe she could take cooking lessons from Ellen.

Maybe she could try again.

Jed spent most of the night debating his choices. He was in love with Beth Kennedy. He could finally admit it. But she didn't love him.

So he could stay here and be miserable, wanting her but not able to have her. Or he could move on down the road, as he'd always done, keeping his focus on finding his own place.

The dream of having a home, a permanent home, had kept him going through the bad times. But now, that dream had no power, because he'd found a new dream.

He wanted Beth.

Maybe if he found a ranch in the area.

That idea brought him upright in his bed. That was a possibility. The area around Wichita Falls was centrally located. He could draw in a lot of customers for his training expertise.

And he'd be close enough to see Beth occasionally. Maybe get her used to the idea of having him around. He lay back down, picturing himself as a ranch owner, a member of the community, a neighbor.

He'd be on a friendly basis with the Kennedy women. He'd see them at all the local functions. He could exchange casual greetings with them like all the other men.

He sat back up in bed.

That wasn't what he wanted.

He wanted the right to draw Beth into his arms, to hold her through the night, to be the father of her children. That thought gave him the enchanting picture of Beth holding a baby, beaming up at him.

He lay back down, enjoying that thought, until he returned to his problem. He didn't want to be a neighbor. He wanted to be a husband.

Sitting back up in bed, he contemplated walking into a church with Beth on his arm.

"Damn, boy, what are you? A yo-yo?" Floyd asked in the dark.

Jed lay back down. "Sorry, Floyd," he whispered. He hadn't realized his movement had awakened his old friend.

"Say, Floyd, when I buy my own place, are you going to come work for me?"

Jed was surprised by the lengthy silence that followed his question. Maybe Floyd had already gone back to sleep.

Then Floyd spoke. "Sorry, Jed, I can't do that."

"Why?"

"'Cause I'm hoping to hang around here long enough for Ellen to take me on.''

"You mean you want to marry her?''

"In a New York minute. She's the sweetest thing I've ever seen.''

Floyd's voice sounded dreamy in the darkness. But Jed could understand the emotion. "Don't blame you, then. Good luck.''

He punched his pillow and turned over. Okay, so being a neighbor wouldn't be enough. But it would be a start. He'd begin looking for a place tomorrow.

Just five days until her first race.

Beth looked for the excitement she'd thought she'd feel. She'd planned on this event a long time. But instead of being excited, she dreaded it.

Because she thought Jed would leave when it was over.

She tried to change things. She added a touch of makeup each morning, trying to enhance her best features. She didn't cake it on, like Sissy, but she added a little lipstick, some mascara.

Jed didn't appear to notice.

She bought some new shirts in soft pastel colors.

She caught him looking at her, but he didn't say anything. He just turned away.

And he'd left the ranch several days during the week. Oh, he was back in time for her training, but he never said where he disappeared to.

On Wednesday, she went into Tumbleweed after lunch. The feed store there had the satin shirts barrel racers wore. It was time to choose her outfit. She was tempted by a raspberry-sherbet color, but then she put on the kelly-green one.

"Oh, Beth, that's the one," the store owner's wife assured her. "It makes your eyes look huge."

Beth stared at herself in the mirror. She didn't picture her racing around the barrels in the shirt. She pictured Jed staring at her in admiration.

"Great. I'll take it."

"How about a new hat?"

Beth stared ruefully at her black Stetson. Aunt Beulah had insisted on good headgear, but they hadn't gotten new ones very often. Beth had worn this hat for a long time.

"I guess it is a little grimy."

"Yeah, and a cream-colored one would look great with your dark hair and that shirt."

Next she tried on some cream jeans to match the hat, and then some new boots, with the carving of an eagle, inset in green leather.

"You're pretty as a picture, Beth. Even if you don't win the race, I reckon you'll win a few cowboys' hearts," the lady assured her.

"Thank you, Mrs. Kessler."

But she didn't want a lot of hearts. Only one.

She hurried home with her purchases, eager to show Jed, to see if any interest sparked in his eyes. But he wasn't there.

Ellen was in the kitchen when she entered the house. "Oh, Beth, Jed called and said for you to go ahead and work out. He'd be here as soon as he could make it.''

Suddenly all her enthusiasm from her shopping trip disappeared. ''Did he say where he was?''

''No, hon, he didn't. What's in all the packages?''

''Oh. Nothing important,'' she said as she trudged through the kitchen and up the stairs.

The ranch Jed had gone to see didn't suit him.

''Don't you have anything listed closer to the Circle K?'' he asked, staring at the Realtor.

''Not really. This place is on a good road, closer to Wichita Falls. Tumbleweed doesn't have all the amenities of a big city.'' The man smiled ingratiatingly.

''I don't like big cities,'' Jed said stoically, and walked back toward his truck. It was already after three. Beth would be on Shorty, racing around the barrels. What if she fell again?

A sense of urgency spurred him on.

''Mr. Davis? There's a small place, a farm really, across the road from the Circle K. A Mrs. Wisner called last week. I haven't had a chance to check it out, but one of my compatriots listed it.''

''Ellen's place?'' Jed asked, surprised. ''How big is it?''

''Just a hundred and fifty acres. That's why I hadn't mentioned it.''

True, he'd asked for a larger place, but he really didn't need the acreage for his training. Less money invested in land meant more money he could put into the facilities.

Right across the road from Beth.

"I want to see it."

"I'll call the office, see if I can get permission to go there now," the man eagerly offered.

"No. I don't have time today. I'll call you tomorrow."

He had to get back to Beth today. But if he bought Ellen's place, he'd be on Beth's doorstep permanently.

Not as close as he wanted, but close enough to give his dreams a chance.

The training went well that afternoon. Jed got there after she and Shorty had been practicing a while, but when he pulled out the stopwatch and timed her, he heaped praise on how well she was doing.

Things had changed this week. They weren't quite as tense around each other as they had been before Saturday night. And Jed talked to her more.

They weren't the best of friends, but then friendship wasn't what Beth had in mind. She managed to get closer to him than he'd let her before. Once or twice, she even bumped into him, hoping he'd think those touches were accidental.

She just had to convince him that a home, a place to stay forever, was more attractive than moving on. Cowboys were notorious for never staying in one place too long.

"Too bad you won't see spring around here," Beth said casually as she unsaddled Shorty. "It's really beautiful."

"Yeah, I've heard. They call it Tornado Alley, don't they?" he teased with a grin.

She almost forgot to respond, so entranced was she with his smile. "Well, we do occasionally have a tornado, but I've never actually been in one."

"I'm glad to hear it," he said, and walked into the barn.

Beth sighed. He did that a lot lately. Acted friendly and then hurried away.

He came back out of the barn, a couple of brushes in hand, and she realized he was going to help her tend to Shorty. Handing her a brush, he began to work on the other side of the horse.

"I bought a shirt for the rodeo today."

He never looked up. "What color?"

"Green. And some cream pants and a new Stetson."

"You'd better take first place or you'll go in the hole on this race. Prize money isn't all that much."

Beth straightened from her brushing and stared at him over Shorty's back. "I'm not racing for the money. I want to win, to show everyone that I have some talent, too."

"Sweetheart—I mean, Beth, you have a lot of talent. You don't need a blue ribbon to prove that."

"But you think I can win?" She held her breath for his response.

"Oh, yeah. You're good enough to go to Nationals

next year if you pursue it. But it's a hard life, following the rodeo circuit. I'm not sure you'll like it."

Here was her opportunity. "You're probably right. Home is pretty important to me."

He didn't say anything.

"Have you ever wanted a home? I mean, a permanent place?"

"That hasn't been an option in the past." He straightened. "You about finished? I'll turn him out. Ellen will have dinner ready in a few minutes."

Washing up for dinner, she cautioned herself to be patient. Jed wasn't used to the idea of a home. She'd have to work on the idea.

Only she didn't think she had much time.

When they were all seated around the table, Abby, after asking the blessing, leaned forward and spoke to Jed.

"I heard a rumor about you today, Jed."

He gave her a cautious look, and Beth stared at first her sister and then Jed. What was Abby talking about?

"What rumor?" he asked.

"I heard you're looking for a place to buy in the area. What do you have in mind?"

Beth's head jerked around to stare at Jed.

"I'm going to set up a training center. This area is centrally located. I thought I should look around. I'd like to put down roots."

Okay. He was willing to put down roots. The only problem was he didn't want her. Just roots.

Chapter Twelve

There was a babble of voices as several people had questions. Jed noticed Beth wasn't one of them. After one stricken look in his direction, she kept her head down.

She didn't want him to stay. Not even as a neighbor. His stomach hurt with the anxiety he felt.

"What have you looked at?" Abby finally managed to ask.

Everyone quieted for his answer. "Nothing I've liked. I really wanted something close by, but the ranch I saw today was almost into Wichita Falls."

He considered his next words, but he decided to go ahead. Maybe Beth would show some approval. "Actually, I heard of another place today. I think it might do."

More questions.

Jed held up his hand. Then he looked at Ellen,

hoping his words didn't upset her. "Your farm, Ellen."

She blushed, but her eyes lit up.

Floyd, however, frowned. "You're selling your place?"

"Yes. Melissa and I have talked about me staying here after she gets well. She has some interesting plans and—"

"She does?" Abby and Beth both asked, surprise on their faces.

"Oh, dear, I didn't mean to spill any secrets."

Jed kept his gaze on Beth's face. Seemed he was causing her more worry.

"But don't you want to keep your own place?" Floyd asked.

"I can't keep it in good shape, Floyd. Even the house is in need of repairs I can't do or afford to have done. I'll get more for it if I sell it now, before it gets too bad, than I will later." She turned her attention to Jed. "But it's not very big."

"The agent said it was a hundred and fifty acres."

"Yes. And it's good land, if someone will take care of it."

He smiled at her. "I can do that. And I don't need a lot of land unless I'm running cattle. With less land, I'll have more money to build better facilities. That's the most important thing in the training game."

"Sounds like you've given this a lot of thought," Abby said.

Jed looked directly at Beth. "I've been on my own

for a long time. I'd like to have my own place, a home I don't have to leave.''

"Well, we'll certainly welcome you to the neighborhood," Abby said, but Jed noticed she took a quick glance at her sister.

Everyone chimed in except Beth.

"Are you going to look at it tomorrow?" Ellen asked. Before he could answer, she added, "I'm not being pushy, I promise. I'm just—anxious."

Floyd patted her hand. "Honey, you couldn't be pushy if you tried."

She smiled at him, but then she turned back to Jed.

"The agent promised he'd call me tonight after he talked to the listing agent. I'm hoping to see it right after lunch tomorrow. I thought maybe Beth would go with me."

Those words got her attention. "Me? Why?"

Because it's not my dream without you. He couldn't say those words, especially not with an audience. He cleared his throat, hoping to contain his emotions. "To give me the woman's perspective."

Barney, who sat next to him, slapped him on the shoulder. "You old dog. You planning on finding a lady and starting a family, ain't you?"

Beth turned deathly pale, jumped up and raced for the stairs.

Jed waited until he got the call from the real estate agent, setting the appointment for one o'clock the next afternoon. Then he returned to the house.

Abby answered the back door. "Hi, Jed. Do you need to see Ellen?"

"No, the appointment is set for tomorrow."

"Oh, good." She held the door open and invited him in. "Cup of coffee?"

"Uh, yeah, thanks."

Soon they were both seated at the kitchen table, cups of hot coffee in front of them. An awkward silence filled the room.

"Uh, Abby, is Beth okay?" There, he'd broached the subject closest to his heart.

"She's fine. Said she had a touch of the flu and thought she was going to embarrass herself."

It took courage to meet Abby's gaze. "Uh, maybe that's true, but—but I think she's upset that I'm staying."

Abby dropped her gaze. "Is the training not going well?"

"The training's fine. But we have a few problems."

"Ah. So you really came to talk to Beth?"

He swallowed. "Do you think she'll come down?"

"I'll go ask."

He sat there, wondering how he could possibly tell her his feelings, when she'd already shown him she was unhappy that he was staying. Maybe tonight he should just aim for getting her to agree to go with him. Tomorrow he could talk about the future.

"Abby said you wanted to see me," Beth said, standing by the door, not approaching the table.

He stood. "I've got an appointment at one tomorrow to see Ellen's place. Will you go with me?"

"Don't you think Ellen would be a better choice? She knows about housekeeping."

He took a step closer to her, his heart sinking as she tensed. "I don't think she'll be objective."

Her teeth sank into her full bottom lip and he yearned to kiss her. "She's—she's very anxious to sell."

"I know. I'm anxious to buy if it'll work at all."

"You are?"

"Yeah. But I need some help. Will you come with me?"

She nibbled on that lip, not looking at him.

"If you come, I'll be able to make a quicker decision, put Ellen out of her misery." It was the only incentive he could think of to get her to come.

Abruptly she said, "Okay."

"You will?"

"Yes, for Ellen. She's—she's going to stay with us."

"Yes." He took another step closer, then halted as she inched toward the door.

"Are you feeling okay?"

Her cheeks bloomed with embarrassment. "I'm fine."

"Okay. Then I'll see you in the morning."

"Yes."

"Thanks for agreeing to go with me." Then he turned and left the house before he said something that upset her again, like I love you.

* * *

Beth made it through her training the next morning. In fact, she had her best time ever. Jed praised her when she pulled Shorty to a halt.

"Incredible, Beth! If you can do that in Ponca City, you'll take first place for sure."

She gave him her best smile, which probably wasn't very good. Any desire to race had disappeared from her head. She knew she could do well. With Shorty, and Jed's training, she could compete.

But did she want to?

Before she could answer that question herself, much less say anything to Jed, he turned away. "You can run through the course a couple more times if you want, but I'm going to put my other horses through their paces. I'll keep an eye out for you in case you run into trouble."

"No. I—I think I'll go in and visit with Melissa before lunch, since I'll be away later."

He nodded but said nothing else.

She wanted to scream at him, to know who would occupy his new home with him. She didn't think it was anyone he'd met since he'd come here. So she assumed he'd had plans before they'd met.

Just her luck.

But she wasn't going to leave her family, her home, because she'd fallen in love with a man who didn't want her. That would be throwing out the baby with the bathwater. Aunt Beulah had warned against such foolishness.

But it was going to hurt.

Especially if he was at the end of their long drive-way.

She'd thought about going this afternoon and telling him he shouldn't buy the farm, that it wouldn't work for whatever woman he had in mind. But she couldn't do that to Ellen.

After lunch, Jed led her to his pickup.

"We're meeting the agent there. His name is Carl Brown. Know him?"

"Yes. His wife was my tenth-grade English teacher."

Jed grinned. "That's part of the charm of living in one place for a long time. You know everyone."

"Yeah, it's a charm, all right, unless you want to get away with something."

Jed's grin widened. "I think that would help parents trying to raise teens."

Beth grimaced. "I guess so, but it doesn't seem fair sometimes."

He came to a halt at the end of the driveway, looked both ways and pulled into Ellen's driveway. It wasn't as long as the Circle K's and they reached the house in no time. They were ahead of the Realtor.

Jed sat behind the steering wheel, staring at the house. "What do you think?"

"I've always liked the house. I've been in it before. It could use some updating, of course, but it has—character."

"Yeah," he agreed with another grin.

He was certainly happy today. Probably because he was thinking of the woman he loved.

"Who is she?" Beth asked abruptly.

He turned to stare at her, frowning. "Who?"

"The woman you're planning a future with."

A horn honked behind them, letting them know the Realtor had arrived.

Beth knew she wouldn't get an answer out of Jed now, but she'd decided she would have her answer before the sun set. No point in prolonging the misery.

First Carl took them through the house. "It's a sturdy building. A little out-of-date, but some paint and wallpaper would take care of that."

"And another bath or two," Jed said, smiling wryly at Beth.

She agreed with him, but the rooms were nice-sized. The kitchen could use an update, too. Not that she was an expert on kitchens.

"Do you want me to drive the acreage with you? There's a creek on the property and several stock tanks. I've got a map here."

Jed and Carl pored over the map, talking about the land, and Beth stood to one side. Then Jed suggested he drive with Carl giving directions.

"I can wait here," Beth suggested, her gaze fixed on Jed's face.

"Nope, you need to come with us." He took her arm and led her to the driver's side of the truck. "Slide in under the wheel."

She did so, but she wondered if he remembered the ride back from Oklahoma when they'd bought Shorty. Sitting in such close quarters had built a lot of tension between them.

He slid in after her, not hesitating to press against her. She scooted over hurriedly. Though with Carl Brown, not a small man, on the other side of her, she didn't have too far to go.

They drove to the edge of the creek. Jed got out and held the door for Beth. Then he took her hand and led her to the creek's edge. "Does this dry up in the summer?"

"No," she assured him. "It's spring-fed."

"Good," he said with a smile, squeezing her fingers, sending a shiver through her body. She loved his big, strong hands. Working hands.

Next they drove to the two stock tanks, checking out the windmill standing above a deep well, and looked at the fenced pastures.

When they pulled to a halt beside the house again, Jed leaned forward to look past Beth. "I'll take it, Mr. Brown."

"All right, Jed. Now, we'll need to negotiate a price. What would you like your initial offer to be?"

"What she's asking."

Beth, as well as Carl Brown, stared at Jed.

"You don't want to dicker?" the agent asked with a frown.

"It's a fair price, and I don't want anything to hold up the sale."

"Well, that's fine. That's just fine. Now, I can arrange the financing for you, so we can close in about four weeks." The man's enthusiasm was mounting.

"No financing. At least not right now. I'm offering

cash," Jed said, his gaze roving over the house and land. Beth could see a look of possession on his face.

However disappointed she was that she wouldn't be the one sharing this home with Jed, she was happy for him. The hunger for a place of his own was there to see.

Carl Brown's jaw sagged and he stared at Jed. "No—no financing? You're paying cash?"

"I've been saving and investing since I started rodeoing, almost fifteen years ago. I don't want a debt hanging over my head."

Carl beamed. "Jed Davis, it is a pleasure doing business with you." He reached for the door handle on his side. "I'll step over to my car and call the listing agent. I should have an answer in about five minutes, if the owner can be reached."

After Carl had closed the door behind him, Jed said, "I think the owner can be reached, don't you?"

Beth laughed, happy for both Ellen and Jed. "I think she's probably sitting by the phone, scarcely breathing."

"Yeah."

"But someone should yell at you about wasting your money."

"Wasting my money? Don't you think the place is worth it?"

"Yes, but you could've bargained," she pointed out. "I remember someone telling me you had to be careful about being taken."

"This situation is different," he assured her, though he suspected she was teasing him.

Suddenly realizing she was still pressed against him for no reason, she started to scoot over. His arm came around her shoulders and held her in place.

"You asked me a question earlier."

She knew at once what question he meant. Steeling herself to hear about the girl he'd left behind, the one he was bringing here to share his life, she nodded.

"I don't know if she'll have me yet. I haven't actually asked her."

Fighting the urge to bury her face in his chest, Beth stared straight ahead. "I see. When—when are you going to ask her?"

"I want to ask her as soon as possible. But I upset her. I don't think she's happy with me."

"If—if she loves you, she'll forgive you."

"Yeah. That's the problem. I'm not sure she cares."

They sat there in silence. Suddenly Beth pushed out of his arms and scooted away from him. "We need to go."

She'd forgotten all about Carl Brown. His appearance at the truck window had her squeaking in surprise.

"Good news! Mrs. Wisner accepted your offer, of course. We can have the papers drawn up and ready for signing in a week, if that's okay with you, Jed. Mrs. Wisner said she has no problem with you taking possession now, if you want."

"Thanks, Carl," Jed said, and reached across Beth

through the window to shake the man's hand. "I appreciate your help."

Carl took himself off, a smile on his face.

"Well, we should get back," Beth said, scooting all the way over to the opposite door.

"Afraid you'll miss training time?"

She ducked her head, then lifted her chin and stared straight ahead. "No. I've decided not to race Saturday."

Jed had been reaching for the keys to start the truck. Now he let his hand fall and stared at her. "What? But you're going to win. It's what you wanted."

"I've changed my mind."

"Well, if you're a quitter, you sure couldn't make it on the rodeo circuit."

His words reminded her of her challenge when he'd threatened to leave once. Unfortunately, she didn't think the outcome would be the same. She said nothing but nodded in agreement.

"Sweetheart, what's wrong? Why did you change your mind?"

Sweetheart. How she loved hearing him call her that. But he shouldn't. "If you're going to ask your lady to forgive you, you shouldn't call me that."

"It looks like she won't forgive me, even if I ask."

She stared at him. "Why do you think that? A few minutes ago, you seemed to think she would."

"That was before she fired me as her trainer."

* * *

Jed didn't feel very good about his chances now. She didn't want any part of him, even his expertise. He turned to stare out the side window, not wanting to see rejection on her face.

When she said nothing, he finally turned to face her. She was staring at him, her hazel eyes wide, a burgeoning hope in them that made his heart stop beating.

"Me?" she whispered.

He couldn't speak. There was too much at stake. But he managed to nod once.

"But you said no!" she said, challenging him.

He didn't have any trouble figuring out what she meant. Those minutes in the pasture had lived in his head every minute since he'd sent her away.

"Sweetheart, you took me by surprise. I wanted you, but I didn't think I should—I'd always kept a strict separation between my business and—"

"And pleasure?" she asked, scooting a few inches toward him.

"Oh, yeah, pleasure," he agreed, his face reflecting that pleasure.

"What changed your mind?" she asked, watching him closely.

"Well, a lot of wanting. But when that cowboy plastered himself all over you, I decided I would be better for you. It took some adjustment since I don't know much about families. I told you I never stayed anywhere long. You might not trust me to—I swear I'd never leave you, if you'll only give me a chance.

But I was afraid you'd think I wouldn't be good enough—"

She didn't let him finish that thought. In a flash, she was back beside him, stopping his words with her hand. "Don't ever say that again."

He removed her hand, replacing it with her lips. After a kiss that almost had him forgetting where they were, he whispered, "Beth, will you marry me? Will you teach me about families, about having a home?"

"Oh, yes," she assured him, then returned to the kissing, an occupation to which Jed had no objection. Until, that is, he feared completely losing control.

"Sweetheart, we've got to call a halt, or we'll be in trouble."

She sent him a saucy look, the likes of which he hadn't seen in several weeks. "You're not going to turn me down this time, are you, Jed Davis?"

He tucked a curl behind her ear, then traced his fingers down her cheek. "Sweetheart, once we're married, I'll never deny you anything. But we've waited this long. I'd kind of like to wait until we marry."

She gave him an outraged look and he hurried on. "Now, don't go thinking I don't want you. It wouldn't take a rocket scientist to know that I do. But my mother—my dad never married her. He took off before I was even born. She was so unhappy. I want to do everything right. I want a marriage that will last for the rest of our lives."

"Then I think we'd better get married very soon,

Jed. Because I can appreciate your feelings...but I'm not willing to wait forever.''

Lord have mercy, neither was he. He scooped her up against his chest and showed her they were in agreement.

Epilogue

Beth rode in the Ponca City rodeo after all. Her personal trainer stood by the entry to the arena, watching her race against the clock. He turned out to be a talented prognosticator when she took first place.

Beth slid off Shorty's back into his arms. "I did it, Jed, I did it!"

"You sure did, sweetheart!" He kissed her, a brief salute, almost chaste, since they were in public.

She pouted, "That wasn't much of a kiss from my future husband."

"Later," he promised. Almost immediately they were surrounded by Abby, friends and neighbors. Jed stood away, letting Beth take the compliments, but she insisted on pulling him back to the center of attention.

Sissy Stallings stalked by, a frown on her face.

When she saw Jed, she came to a halt. "I don't care what she paid you. I'll double your fee."

Jed grinned down at Beth. Then he nodded to Sissy. "I appreciate the offer, but I'm afraid I can't accept."

"Why not? I just told you I'd double the amount."

Jed smiled. "I can't, because I'm marrying Beth. I'll be her permanent trainer. Until she retires from barrel racing, I won't be training anybody else."

Outraged, Sissy stomped away. But his announcement received a much happier reception among the circle around them. Congratulations rang out.

Beth leaned against him and Jed wrapped his arms around her. Even in Ponca City, miles from his new place, Jed Davis had come home.

Home to Beth. Wherever she was, his heart would be. And together, they would build a future.

* * * * *

Don't miss THE BORROWED GROOM
(Silhouette Romance #1457)
on sale July 2000.
Melissa Kennedy soon finds she needs a
fiancé and quick—and handsome ranch
foreman Rob Hansen is more than willing to
apply for the job!

If you enjoyed what you just read,
then we've got an offer you can't resist!

Take 2 bestselling
love stories FREE!
Plus get a FREE surprise gift!

Clip this page and mail it to Silhouette Reader Service™

IN U.S.A.
3010 Walden Ave.
P.O. Box 1867
Buffalo, N.Y. 14240-1867

IN CANADA
P.O. Box 609
Fort Erie, Ontario
L2A 5X3

YES! Please send me 2 free Silhouette Romance® novels and my free surprise gift. Then send me 6 brand-new novels every month, which I will receive months before they're available in stores. In the U.S.A., bill me at the bargain price of $2.90 plus 25¢ delivery per book and applicable sales tax, if any*. In Canada, bill me at the bargain price of $3.25 plus 25¢ delivery per book and applicable taxes**. That's the complete price and a savings of at least 10% off the cover prices—what a great deal! I understand that accepting the 2 free books and gift places me under no obligation ever to buy any books. I can always return a shipment and cancel at any time. Even if I never buy another book from Silhouette, the 2 free books and gift are mine to keep forever. So why not take us up on our invitation. You'll be glad you did!

215 SEN C24Q
315 SEN C24R

Name	(PLEASE PRINT)	
Address	Apt.#	
City	State/Prov.	Zip/Postal Code

* Terms and prices subject to change without notice. Sales tax applicable in N.Y.
** Canadian residents will be charged applicable provincial taxes and GST.
  All orders subject to approval. Offer limited to one per household.
  ® are registered trademarks of Harlequin Enterprises Limited.

SROM00_R   ©1998 Harlequin Enterprises Limited

Multi-*New York Times* bestselling author

NORA ROBERTS

knew from the first how to capture readers' hearts.
Celebrate the 20th Anniversary of Silhouette Books
with this special 2-in-1 edition containing her fabulous
first book and the sensational sequel.

Coming in June

IRISH HEARTS

Adelia Cunnane's fiery temper sets proud, powerful horse
breeder Travis Grant's heart aflame and he resolves to
make this wild *Irish Thoroughbred* his own.

Erin McKinnon accepts wealthy Burke Logan's loveless
proposal, but can this ravishing *Irish Rose* win her
hard-hearted husband's love?

Also available in June from
Silhouette Special Edition (SSE #1328)

IRISH REBEL

In this brand-new sequel to *Irish Thoroughbred*, Travis and
Adelia's innocent but strong-willed daughter Keeley discovers
love in the arms of a charming Irish rogue with a talent for
horses...and romance.

Silhouette®
Where love comes alive™

Look Who's Celebrating Our 20th Anniversary:

"Happy 20th birthday, Silhouette. You made the writing dream of hundreds of women a reality. You enabled us to give [women] the stories [they] wanted to read and helped us teach [them] about the power of love."

—*New York Times* bestselling author
Debbie Macomber

"I wish you continued success, Silhouette Books.... Thank you for giving me a chance to do what I love best in all the world."

—International bestselling author
Diana Palmer

"A visit to Silhouette is a guaranteed happy ending, a chance to touch magic for a little while.... It refreshes and revitalizes and makes us feel better.... I hope Silhouette goes on forever."

—Award-winning bestselling author
Marie Ferrarella

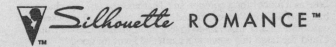

COMING NEXT MONTH

#1456 FALLING FOR GRACE—Stella Bagwell
An Older Man
The moment Jack Barrett saw his neighbor, he wanted to know everything about her. Soon he learned beautiful Grace Holliday was pregnant and alone…and too young for him. He also found out she needed protection—from *his* jaded heart....

#1457 THE BORROWED GROOM—Judy Christenberry
The Circle K Sisters
One thing held Melissa Kennedy from her dream of running a foster home—she was single. Luckily, her sexy ranch foreman, Rob Hanson, was willing to be her counterfeit fiancé, but could Melissa keep her borrowed groom…forever?

#1458 DENIM & DIAMOND—Moyra Tarling
Kyle Masters was shocked when old friend Piper Diamond asked him to marry her. He wasn't looking for a wife, yet how could he refuse when without him, she could lose custody of her unborn child? It also didn't hurt that she was a stunning beauty....

#1459 THE MONARCH'S SON—Valerie Parv
The Carramer Crown
One minute she'd washed ashore at the feet of a prince, the next, commoner Allie Carter found herself "companion" to Lorne de Marigny's son…and falling for the brooding monarch. He claimed his heart was off-limits, yet his kisses suggested something else!

#1460 JODIE'S MAIL-ORDER MAN—Julianna Morris
Bridal Fever!
Jodie Richards was sick of seeking Mr. Right, so she decided to marry her trustworthy pen pal. But when she went to meet him, she found his brother, Donovan Masters, in his place. And with one kiss, her plan for a passionless union was in danger....

#1461 LASSOED!—Martha Shields
Pose as a model for a cologne ad? That was the *last* job champion bull-rider Tucker Reeves wanted. That is, until a bull knocked him out…and Tucker woke up to lovely photographer Cassie Burch. Could she lasso this cowboy's hardened heart for good?

CMN0600